About the Author

Jane Stemp writes: 'I was born in Lewisham in 1961 and grew up in Surrey. I have cerebral palsy, and spent much of my childhood and early teens in hospital. I took a degree in English at Somerville College, Oxford, then trained as a librarian in Aberystwyth. I have worked in Oxford since 1987, but live (with my pet hamster) in Caversfield, near Bicester.

I started writing when I was eleven, *Waterbound*, my first published novel, was shortlisted for the National Association for Special Educational Needs Children's Book Award. I have been involved in disability rights campaigning, and also enjoy archaeology, cathedrals, cooking (and eating) historical recipes, and music.

Secret Songs

Jane Stemp

Hodder
Children's
Books

a division of Hodder Headline plc

First published in Great Britain in 1997
by Hodder Children's Books

A Catalogue record for this book is available
from the British Library

ISBN 0 340 68160 8

Typeset by Avon Dataset Ltd, Bidford-on-Avon, Warks

Printed and bound in Great Britain by
Mackays of Chatham, Chatham, Kent

Hodder Children's Books
A Division of Hodder Headline PLC
338 Euston Road
London NW1 3BH

For Sara, Mary and Nic:
not forgetting
Ed, Val and 'Sally'

Acknowledgements: thanks to Jim Cole of S. H. Jones,
Bicester, and Sergeant John Thurston of Bicester
Police, for information provided.

One

Ceri tucked her hair back, and with the same movement slid the hearing aid out of her left ear and into the pocket of her jeans. A sharp jab in her back meant that Sam, in the seat behind her, had seen her do it, but with any luck he wouldn't give her away. Half an hour ago Mum had told him not to say another word until they were in Scotland.

She looked at her mother out of the corner of her eyes. Mum had her driving face on, lips clamped shut, frowning slightly whenever she overtook: but there was just a chance that she would notice if Ceri took the other aid out, so Ceri went for the next-best option and turned it off with another flick of her hair. A good thing she'd had it cut, there weren't so many excuses for fiddling with your hair when it was braided back. With the hand that was in her pocket Ceri fingered the small, hard thing curled shell-like in her palm. She wasn't supposed – wasn't allowed – to take her hearing aids out when she was awake: Mum had decided that she, Ceri, had to be kept in touch with the real world. But Ceri would rather keep in touch with her real ears, the ones that didn't work properly.

The motorway roared under the car tyres, masking the faint high hissing that was perpetually in her ears. They were going on holiday; having a relaxing break, or that was what Mum and Michael had said. But while Ceri was packing last night Sam had come in, bounced on the bed, and said, 'There's going to be trouble. I bet you.'

Ceri looked up. 'On holiday?'

Sam snorted. 'Oh, you and me, we're just bolt-on holiday extras. Dad doesn't want Ruth thinking Mum's gone all the way to Scotland just to see her. *And* he doesn't see why Mum should. I bet something's going on.'

'What's Michael got to do with it? He isn't even related to her – Ruth.'

'Dad? Nothing, Mum just wants him along.'

'How do you know all this, anyway?' Ceri said, wrapping her favourite cassettes in bubble-wrap and sliding them down the side of the suitcase.

'Overheard them shouting in the kitchen.'

'Lucky you,' Ceri said, and then hoped she hadn't sounded too sarcastic. So Sam could overhear things and she couldn't – great deal, not. Only sometimes, sometimes: it was easy to resent Sam's casual acceptance of his own luck.

Luck has nothing to do with it. Ceri had shaken the fledgling argument out of her head, flashed Sam a quick smile, and got on with her packing.

And then, whatever was going on, Mum had to bring Ceri and Sam on her own after all, because Michael – Sam's father, but not Ceri's – was called out at short notice to his firm's head office in Holland.

The noise of the car and the wind through the open sun roof

made a noise like an eternally-falling wave. Ceri always said she could hear musical notes in it, but nobody ever believed her, and lately she had given up telling them. She squinted over her right shoulder. Sam was curled up in his own world of sound. The wires of his personal stereo snaked up into his fair hair, and he was nudging her back inadvertently as he marked the beat with one foot.

Ruth. Ceri had seen Ruth now and again, when she came to tea at their flat in London. She remembered a bright, burnished girl, who had stood laughing in the sunshine on their balcony one Easter; Ceri had wished her own hair was that shade of auburn, instead of black. Ruth was American, but had come to England to study; and she had been doing summer work in Scotland for what seemed like years.

However much or little Michael had to do with it, Ceri's mother didn't have much more. She was Ruth's stepmother, the way Sam's father was now Ceri's stepfather: marriages breaking and reforming as partners in the dance let go of each other's hands and took hold again. Bonds dissolving like chemicals. If only it was as much fun as a dance. If only it was as logical as chemistry.

Ceri had been born in America, a little more than fifteen years ago. When she was three, Mum had got divorced and brought Ceri back to England with her. But why? Ceri thought, and why will nobody tell me why? She could hardly remember the time before Mum had married Michael Hughes, Sam's father: she could only just remember the arrival of Sam. A lot of her early memories had disappeared into the fog of being ill, along with some of her hearing.

Letters from Ruth arrived sometimes, thin blue paper with

strange stamps. Christmas and birthday cards too. Never anything from Ceri's father. Their father. Paul Schaefer, the one definite thing she had in common with Ruth. Ceri could not remember him at all. Mum wouldn't talk about him, and Ceri had never got Ruth on her own to ask. But once she had been reading a book of Mum's, and a photograph had fallen out: or to be correct, two bits, torn across. On the back was written just, 'Jen from Paul'. Ceri kept the half with his face. It was blurred, and he had been facing into the sun when the photograph was taken, so she couldn't really see what he looked like, although his hair was dark. Maybe he looked like her.

Ceri moved her head a little, and looked at her mother, still staring straight ahead except for an occasional glance at the rear mirror. She sighed, closed her eyes, listened again for the music in the noise of the engine and began to conduct the orchestra, invisible in her head. In a little while she fell asleep.

She woke up in a car park full of coaches. 'Where are we?'

'Gretna Green,' Sam said loudly in her right ear.

'I thought we weren't going to stop here.' That had been what most of the argument had been about, once they were past Carlisle.

'Mum had to. Too much coffee at lunch.' Sam stared out of the window. 'Actually, now I see it,' he said, 'I don't know why I wanted to.'

'What's that noise?' Ceri asked. There were a lot of noises, all blowing into her right ear like a gale as soon as she flicked the switch on her hearing aid; but this one was strange.

Sam was better than either Michael or Mum at realising what exactly caught Ceri's ears. He twisted round to look out of the rear window, then faced front again. 'There's some kid howling. I think he dropped his ice-cream. Or there's bagpipes over on the far side, by that building.'

Ceri flipped the shade down from the top of the windscreen and fiddled until she could see out of the rear window in the make-up mirror. 'It's the bagpipes,' she said. 'Weird.'

'Worse than your whale music,' Sam said, grinning.

'You shut up. I like it.' But Ceri looked again. 'Just imagine him underwater with a frog-suit and flippers.'

Sam was still giggling when Mum came back to the car, handed out shortbread, and revved out of the car park like a police car let loose from Hollywood. Sam, who had learnt the manual alphabet to pass messages round the back of his class, spelt out 'Foul mood no Dad' with his hands squashed forward on the left of Ceri's seat where Mum couldn't see. Ceri had learnt the one-handed alphabet from America as well as the two-handed British version from her audiologist, years ago, without Mum's permission. Mum thinks I ought to be part of the world where you wear hearing aids and listen to real conversation. But I prefer music in the engine, and whale voices.

She slid her left hand back through the gap between the seat and the car door and spelt out 'Foul mood him or not these days.' It seemed true enough.

They drove for hours. At home in the south by now it would have been dark: here they seemed to be chasing the day's end beyond the mountains. It was a strange, pearly light, the twilight of a secret land. As they went deeper into it, Ceri dozed again. She opened her eyes sometimes to see mountains, dark shapes moving past outside the car windows. The car swung heavily as the road curved. Once when they were driving downhill she

5

looked out and saw water in front of them; even that dim sky was light enough to reflect off the sea. They stopped, waited on a tarmac slope that pushed out into the water, still and slickly rippled as if the twilight was a sort of oil to calm it.

'Where are we?' Ceri mumbled. Mum reached back for the road atlas, put it on Ceri's lap and pointed. Most of the land was marked white, with thin blue hairlines for streams. Ceri focused her eyes on the strange names: Stob Coire A'Chearchaill, Ardgour, Lochuisge. They were at Corran, marked with a line for a ferry. Mum left the map with Ceri and started the engine again. Down the slope to the ferry, jolt and rattle aboard, and then the strange driving, not-driving feel of being in a car on a boat. It was more like crossing the border than crossing the border had been.

Down in the south the summer had been almost tangible with warmth and leafiness for weeks. Here the edges of things seemed crisp and hard, as though the ghost of winter haunted the country, reminding summer that it was only mortal. Into the crowding mountains they drove, or the car swam maybe: the edges and lines of the slopes moving and falling like waves, in hidden gestures that were too slow and huge to be seen entire and interpreted.

At last they left the tarred road and bumped over rough ground. Ceri roused, and saw a white gate in front of them, and a glimpse of Mum's face as she turned to speak to Sam. Sam opened the car door, slid out, and opened the gate. Slowly the car rolled up to the wall of a long, low, white house. Beyond it Ceri could see another building, not the walls of it, but the shapes of the light shining out from curtained windows. Mum had said they would be staying in a house next to a farm; that must be the farm.

Ceri grabbed the suitcase that Mum handed her, and stumbled drowsily indoors. She went through the door that Mum opened, into a bedroom with a wash-basin in one corner, brushed her teeth automatically, dragged her clothes off and curled up under the duvet.

In the middle of the night she came wide awake, as if someone had touched her face. The moon was shining through the gap between the curtains straight into her eyes. It was full, or maybe just past full. Ceri padded across to the window, her ears still ringing faintly at a deeper pitch than usual, an echo of the motorway. She looked out. Moonlight lay across the water like a path, and in it something moved, turning like a fish under the water, and splashing. Small silent fountains of light followed the seal as it swam across the bay and out of sight, its back rising and falling in smooth curves like a miniature version of the mountain slopes outside the windows of the car.

Next morning it was raining: when Ceri put her hearing aids in and switched them on, the noise filled the world like hiss on the radio, a louder version of her usual noise. She went out of her bedroom, and found that she had come in to the back of the house last night on the upper level. Through a window at the end of the landing she could see, across a farm yard, the building whose windows had been lit the night before. There were hens and a sheepdog, a Border collie in the yard, and another collie lying on the driver's seat of a Land-Rover that had been left with its door open.

The open staircase led down to a big room with a window that filled most of the outside wall. Ceri looked out at the water: any one of the small, choppy waves could have been a seal's head. There was a beach at the end of the lawn, a stippled mass of grey and brown, with the waves heaving like liquid pewter beyond it. The rain blurred everything, and Ceri could hardly see whether there was a shore on the other side of the water; were those faint shapes of hills, or only a swirl in the clouds? She went through another door and found herself in the kitchen, where Mum was rattling out the breakfast things.

'Where's Sam?' Ceri asked.

'Gone for milk for the porridge.'

'I don't like porridge.'

'Don't say that to a Scotsman,' Mum said, and laughed suddenly instead of losing her temper as she usually did when Ceri contradicted her. 'Just this one morning, or there won't be anything else, because I forgot the bread and the cornflakes.'

There was a buffet of wind, and Ceri, who was standing with her back to the outside, felt the vibration through her feet as much as heard the door bang. Sam came in, dripping, his fingers stretched round the tops of four milk bottles. 'The farmer's wife says,' he reported, 'that it's gey dreich. What's her name, and what did she mean?'

'Morag MacInnes,' Mum said. 'Mrs MacInnes to you. I think she said she's from the Borders, and I don't know what she means either. Horrible weather, I should think.'

'Morag or Mrs,' Sam said, 'and wherever she's from, I wish she'd talk my language.'

Ceri had started on Mum's gluey porridge already, without waiting for the milk. While the others were helping themselves she gulped some hot coffee to scour her mouth out, and ran upstairs. Time to unpack: her paintbox, her cassette player, her cassettes.

8

She was kneeling on the floor, intent on the latest painting, when Sam came in and switched the sound off.

'Hey!'

'I only came to say we're going for a drive to see if there are any shops open,' Sam said. 'Trust Mum to forget the bread on a Sunday.' He nudged the cassette case round with his toes. ' "Chansons secrets de baleines". What's that when it's at home?'

'Secret songs of the whales.'

'I don't know why you listen to that stuff. Nobody else does.'

'I like it. I like listening to something that doesn't have to be understood.'

'You're *weird*,' Sam said, and went out. Ceri pressed the switch down. The sound began again, swirling like water. She loaded some green paint onto her brush and pulled it across the paper. Here was where she felt at home, in the undersea country she had been painting for years. Where the twittering sounds of human speech were little and unimportant, because meaning flowed through the water in the tides and currents. Ceri felt that she would never need words there, because none of the sounds needed to be understood: which was why she painted it, because she could never find the right words anyway. And it was there that the whales sang.

'Right,' Mum said later, as they were finishing tea – with bread – 'tonight we're going to a cayley.'

'A what?' Ceri said.

'C-e-i-l-i-d-h. And no objections please.'

'I wasn't objecting. It's a new word.'

Mum looked suddenly apologetic. 'So it is. Sorry, darling, I

9

forgot.' And she took the teapot out for a refill before Ceri could even think of saying, '*Forgot*? But I'm your daughter! How can you forget?'

It was still raining in a blue twilight world when they climbed into the car and bounced off, first over bleak moorlands and then down into dripping woods.

'Is this the way we came?' Ceri asked, and Mum shook her head. 'No. We're heading for –' but she couldn't hear the name. 'Where?'

Mum said the name again; Ceri wondered whether to ask once more, but Sam pulled at her arm from behind. She slid her left hand back, and he spelt it out secretly by touch; a village beyond Strontian.

They came out of the wet darkness into a warm hall that seemed dazzling bright. There was a haze in the air, a layer of blue-grey hovering below the ceiling, as if it was the surface and they were below water. Mum wrinkled her nose. 'So much smoking,' she said.

Ceri sniffed. This was not like the sharp, stinging cigarette smoke that came drifting up from the flat below them in London. She looked round the room; several men were smoking pipes. It was a warm smell, like being indoors on a cold night. 'Smells nicer,' she said.

'Just as bad for you,' her mother replied, as if she had not once been on thirty a day. 'Sam, can you see Morag MacInnes?'

'How should I know?' Sam said. 'I only met her the once.'

'What does she look like?' Ceri asked.

'Little old lady in a flowery apron,' Sam said.

'She won't wear the apron here, stupid!' Mum said. 'Look, there she is. Not particularly little nor particularly old, I'd say.'

A neat, stocky woman in a blue raincoat, with what Ceri thought of as sensible shoes, and grey hair twisted up and pinned at the back of her head, was beckoning them across to the farthest corner. They dodged through the crowd, round chairs apparently scattered at random, and sat down beside Mrs MacInnes. And as far as Ceri could tell, Mrs MacInnes and Mum began almost at once, what dreadful weather it was, what the roads had been like yesterday.

The hall was filling up. People squeezed between the chairs, blocking Ceri's line of sight and cutting her off from the conversation. Someone handed a bottle in front of Sam, and Mum took it and passed it on in a hurry.

'Oh *Mum*!' Sam said.

'What was it anyway?' Ceri asked.

'Whisky,' Mum said, 'and you're both under age.'

'What about you?' Sam said, grinning.

'I hate the taste,' Mum said, looking surprisingly grim. 'I'll see if there's anything else.' When she had gone Morag MacInnes leaned across, tapped Sam's arm, and handed him her glass. 'Quick,' she said, winking, 'before she comes back.'

Sam took a mouthful, swallowed, and made such a face that Ceri burst out laughing. She managed to stop herself by the time Mum came back with some lemonade: it was very sweet, and not very cold, but she drank it all the same, for the feel of the bubbles popping inside her mouth.

There was a lot of hushing and shuffling, and two women came out of a door at the end of the hall. One of them was carrying a harp: not the big concert harp Ceri had sometimes seen on television, but one much smaller. There was an announcement: Ceri couldn't make it out, and turned to Sam, but he shook his head, and sat on his hands to indicate he wasn't talking at the moment. Ceri turned the volume up on her hearing aids.

The music burst on her ears like a waterfall. She had never heard anything like it. It was the perfect music for her undersea country, rippling and flowing like light on the water. Somewhere underneath there were larger, slower sounds that she couldn't hear properly, but perhaps nobody else could either. Hidden words in another language, that someone was speaking to her and her alone. Phrases as significant and unfamiliar as the gestures of the mountain slopes.

Ceri could hardly hear the words to the song itself, and some of them sounded strange, but it hardly seemed to matter. She did hear the first verse.

> 'An earthly nourris sits and sings
>> And aye she sings "Bye lily wean,
>> It's little ken I my bairn's father,
>>> Still less the land where he dwells in." '

When the song was over and everyone was still clapping, Ceri felt a cold draught on the back of her neck. The door had opened. She twisted round in her seat and looked. Just outside, silvered by the lamplight and the rain, stood a girl with red hair. It was Ruth.

Two

Ruth turned her head towards Ceri, and their eyes met. Ruth lifted one hand, close to her face, in a wave that was like a private greeting.

'Look,' Ceri said, and half-rose from her chair. But at that moment, with a noise that reminded Ceri of the sea on a pebble beach, everyone stood up and began pushing their chairs back against the wall. The song had been for a quiet beginning, and now it was time to dance. Ceri tried to push towards the door, but she might as well have waded into a river in flood. For a moment she felt swung away among a torrent of strangers. There was Ruth's face again – Ceri stretched out one arm towards her, and Ruth made a wide, rueful gesture like a shrug, and plunged laughing into the dance herself, mouthing a word which Ceri recognised as, 'Later.' She turned to look for Mum, but was caught up in the dance before she could do anything. The music like water flowed out of her head and was replaced by the springing feel of dancing. She didn't know the steps, but she could watch, and learn; and presently when someone held out their hands she took them and joined in.

When the music stopped again she found she was holding hands with a complete stranger: a boy of her own age, maybe older, with fair hair and freckles and grey eyes. He was too much out of breath to say anything at first: Ceri slipped her hand from his, and wondered whether she should turn the volume up on her hearing aids. But she could almost have guessed his first question anyway.

'Hi. What's your name?'

'Ceri.'

'As in County Kerry?'

'No – C-e-r-i. It's Welsh.'

'You from there?'

'No, I'm from London.' She looked at him. 'Who are you?'

'Fergal MacInnes. Are you one of the people staying at my Uncle John's place? My father farms in the next valley over, we're all in and out of each other's yards mostly.' He smiled cheerfully.

It was a lot of information to take in at once, and he talked fast. All Ceri could think of to say was, 'You don't sound very Scottish.'

'Me? Och, we're a friendly clan, us MacInneses, and I'm aye douce for the Sassenachs,' said Fergal, grinning.

Ceri, not understanding the words exactly, smiled at him: then turned her head as she saw a glint of red hair out of the corner of her eye.

'Oh great – there's Ruth,' Fergal said.

'You know her?'

'She comes here every summer. Works at the Abbey.' He stopped. 'You mean, you know her too?'

'She's my half-sister. I'm not sure I –' Ceri said, but it was

14

too late. Fergal was shouldering his way through the next dance as it formed, and obviously expecting her to follow. Ceri waited a moment, shrugged, and went after him. The crowd opened in front of them, closed again; and when they saw Ruth again she was across the room.

'*Dia*,' said Fergal. 'She's like a will-o'-the-wisp.' He stood still, and waved his hands above his head like someone flagging a helicopter down. 'Ruth! Hey, *Ruth*!'

She saw him then, waved, and came towards them with the easy swinging stride Ceri remembered.

'Well, hello!' she said. 'You are Ceri, aren't you?'

'M-m.' Ceri nodded. The background noise was building up again. She would have to keep her eyes on Ruth's lips.

'Still crazy about unicorns?'

Amazing the things people remembered. Ceri said, 'That was ages ago. I grew up.'

Ruth smiled. 'Ages? It was last year, if I recall. And "grew up" is right, you're a regular beanpole. But what's wrong with unicorns?'

'Nothing,' Ceri said. 'I just rather think about something I might see.' And there are other ways of growing up. Wasn't Ruth going to notice that?

'So?'

'Whales,' Ceri said.

Fergal snorted. 'Not many of those here.'

'I never said there were,' Ceri retorted. 'But I saw a seal last night.'

'Well, seeing we get seals the way other people get rabbits, I'm not surprised.'

Ruth laughed. 'Fergal MacInnes, you want it both ways.'

'Ever know a man who didn't want the last word?' Fergal said, grinning again, and walked off.

'I did not,' Ruth said to herself. Ceri watched her for a moment, trying to work out how she had changed since they last met. She was as tall and slim as ever; it was her clothes that were different. When Ceri had met her before, Ruth had been elegant in smart clothes and make-up. Now she was in jeans and a jacket that seemed to be made of rags and tatters; but she still had that golden, glowing look about her, as if she stood in her own pool of sunshine.

'And now he's gone,' Ruth said suddenly, 'are you going to tell me why you're here?'

Ceri stared at her. 'I don't know what you mean. I came with Mum.'

'Oh sure – and she told you to get nice to Ruth and make her go home.'

'She never said anything!' Ceri found herself looking Ruth straight in the eyes. She must have grown taller if she could do that. 'Nothing,' she repeated. 'What is going on? Sam said something was, but nobody tells me anything, not so I can hear it anyway . . .' Ceri clamped her lips shut and turned away.

After a moment she felt Ruth tapping her shoulder, but refused to turn round. Ruth turned instead, coming to face Ceri.

'I almost forgot about your ears,' she said. 'I'm sorry, OK? Forget I said what I did. I guess your mom just riled me. If she wants me to go home she can at least tell me why, and she won't.'

'Did she tell you "because I said so?" ' Ceri asked.

Ruth smiled. 'More or less. But I like it here. I'm staying.'

'Do you want me to tell her that?'

16

'I just did,' Ruth answered, 'but thanks. Look, Ceri – how long is this vacation of yours?'

'Two weeks. Why?'

Ruth shrugged. 'So I know. You are my kid sister, after all. How about we do some things together?'

'Great,' Ceri said. Ruth had hardly been a sister when they had met before, more like one of Mum's terrifying fashionable business friends. She'd seen Ruth so rarely that it was hard to remember that they shared a surname: strange to have her family extended like this. Only Ceri wasn't sure she liked being called a kid sister.

'Then I'll be seeing you,' Ruth said, touched Ceri lightly on the shoulder and went away into the swirling dance.

Mum came and found her before it all ended, but by then Ceri was so exhausted she didn't much mind. Even Mum was looking cheerful, pink-cheeked and with her fair hair fluffed out of its usual sleekness.

'Where Sam?' Ceri asked, slurring the words together, she was so tired.

'Went back with Morag – Mrs MacInnes,' her mother said. They steered an awkward course together through the dance; looked back once, and saw one slim white arm waving goodbye out of the crowd. Mum waved back, and said, 'Come on, Ceri.'

They found Sam in the kitchen talking to a man who looked quite at home there; a tall bony man with fairish hair going grey.

'I thought I asked you to put the kettle on, Sam,' Mum said, taking her coat off and hanging it up.

'Sorry,' Sam said. 'Forgot.' He picked up the kettle, stared at the water level, and clicked the switch. Ceri saw the subtle movements of Mum's back under the shirt, as she drew breath to say something scathing, and then relaxed and decided not to. Instead she turned round and said, 'Ceri, of course, you haven't met Mr MacInnes. I should have introduced you.'

'Pleased to meet you,' the man said, shaking hands with Ceri. 'You'll have met my nephew, I dare say.'

What had Fergal said? My uncle John. He did look a bit like Fergal, Ceri decided. She smiled and said, 'Pleased to meet you too.'

John MacInnes went out, saying, 'Tomorrow, then,' to Sam, just as the kettle boiled. Ceri drank her hot chocolate as soon as she could, and went up to her room. She knelt for a while beside the window, looking out across the water, but the moon was behind the cloud tonight.

If the seal was there, she did not see it; but something swam through her dreams all night, among the inhabitants of the undersea land with music in its tides.

It was early in the morning when she woke, but someone else was up and about already: when Ceri leaned out of bed and put her hand on the floor she could feel the vibration. No rain this morning, but a fog that was almost as bad. And although there was no point in getting up, Ceri found she couldn't sleep again. Instead she looked at the bookshelves, which were cluttered with a mix of books and tapes that didn't belong to her but to the house. She pulled some of the cassettes down and looked at the inlay cards. One with a picture of a harp. Ceri lay and thought for a while, then rolled out of bed, pulled on a t-shirt and went into Sam's room.

Sam was the person she had felt moving around. He was fully

dressed, with his boots on, and the least lurid of his jackets. Ceri stood in the doorway and said, 'Can I borrow your stereo, Sam?'

'If you don't run the batteries down. Mind out, I'm coming through there.'

She backed out of his way. 'Where are you going?'

'Out with John MacInnes. He might teach me to shoot.'

Ceri made a face, and Sam laughed. 'Lots of fluffy bunnies waiting to be made into dinner.'

'You're horrid, Sam Hughes.'

'So I may be, Ceri Schaefer, but I still lend you my things. Go on, take it.' And he clomped out, Frankenstein-footed in his enormous boots.

Back in her room, Ceri put 'Chansons secrets de baleines' on her own machine, and the tape she had found on Sam's. After a few moments of fiddling with dials and listening, she had the balance she wanted. The harp-music rose and fell, with the faint, insistent boom and swirl of whales and waves behind it. She looked into the grey beyond the window and unfocussed her eyes, looking back into her dreams.

Down in the undersea country there would be a storm, the green sky whipped into white clouds of foam, and the noise of the pounding waves shaking the ground underfoot. Ceri imagined the people, whoever they were, huddling away back in caves in the rocks, their eyes shining with the reflected light of the foam. When the world was turned around like this, the whales would be far out of reach of the rocks' black teeth. Only when the storm died down, so that the sunbeams came angling through the water, and the current set fair, would they be able to hear the whales singing again.

Ceri shook her head, and came up out of her imagination like a swimmer coming up for air. She looked at her watch: time for breakfast, but no smell of it in the house. She went out of her room and past what she thought of as the inland door. On this side of the house the fog was clearing; the door was a little open, and piled up in that narrow gap was a picture of bare dappled hills and blue sky. Ceri stood and listened, her hands on the walls: no sound or feel of anyone indoors. She went to her mother's room to see if she was still in bed: but the room was empty. Only a letter lay half-written on the dressing-table; blue paper, air mail. With a glance over her shoulder Ceri stepped into the room and looked at it.

. . . *As for Ruth, I always told you she was none of my business and she agrees with me. It seems she has some young man who is her latest acquisition but what is that to do with either of us, and why should she come home because you want her to? Be thankful she is growing up, and leave me alone. I came here for a holiday, because I like Ruth and she's invited us up here before; but I'm only – and reluctantly – meddling in her affairs, which only you asked me to do, to keep you on the other side of the Atlantic where you belong. I won't give you my home address, and I don't care to be contacted at the office either, so you may as well stop trying.*

And there the writing broke off. Ceri reached out to turn the letter over. Then a door slammed, and she was out of the room faster than thinking. It had only been the inland door, blowing shut; but then she hadn't needed to see who the letter was to, anyway. It could only be to her father. She leaned back against the wall with her heart thumping. I had no idea they were still in touch. Why didn't she tell me, why doesn't she want me to know, or him to come here? . . . Ceri stood up straight and ran her tongue over her dry lips. Supposing he did come? I might meet him. At last. And be able to ask him, where have you been all my life?

She went downstairs and past the seaward door: under the grey, a sparkle of sunlight. The fog on the water was beginning to lift too.

On the table were boxes of cereal and a note. 'Dear Ceri, I did shout but maybe you were asleep. I've gone for a walk.'

There had been a time, once, when Mum would have come to find her if there was no answer, in case she hadn't heard. There had been a time when she would make Ceri pronounce everything as close to perfectly as possible. And though it was fine enough not being corrected every other minute, sometimes Ceri did wonder if Mum had got tired of caring. Well . . . all to the better. She could do what she liked. Ceri got herself a plateful of all her favourite sorts of cereal, and ate it dry, which she preferred because it sounded better. When she had finished she found a pencil, added 'Me too' to the end of the note, and went out by the sea door.

Three

The sun had come full out by the time she reached the water's edge. Ceri wandered down the beach and sat on a grey boulder that pushed up like an ancient fossil bone from under the shingle. The waves made a music that she could map to the colours and shapes of the pebbles. She sat listening to it for a while, the curve and clash and fall of it; and then a shadow fell across her feet. She looked up quickly to see a stranger standing between her and the sun. He moved round, so that the light fell on his face. 'I did say hallo, but you didn't hear me.'

Now that she could see him, his voice was extraordinarily clear: it seemed to ring inside her head. She said, 'I was thinking.'

He sat down beside her. 'About what?'

What an odd question to ask. And them complete strangers. Ceri moved her head, as if the flight of a gull along the shore had caught her eye, but really to look at him under her lashes. She never had seen him before, she was sure of that. But something about him looked familiar. He had thick dark hair, brushed back from his face. Like a lion's mane, Ceri thought, only he didn't remind her of a lion. He reminded her of . . . she couldn't think what, exactly. Something in the sleekness of his hair, the powerful shoulders. His hair looked wet, as if he had been swimming, and there was a sheen on his skin like water, or dried salt. She wanted to hear his voice again. Had it really been so clear, so easy to understand?

'What your name?' she asked.

He glanced at her, and Ceri realised she must have made some mistake. 'Euan,' he said.

'Just Euan?'

'Usually.' He plunged his hand into the shingle, and brought it up with a white quartz pebble in his palm. 'You could call me Roane if you liked.'

'I'm Ceri.'

He smiled again. 'In Wales Ceri is a man's name.'

Ceri threw a stone, and changed the pattern in the water. 'In my country Ceri is *my* name.'

Euan said seriously, as if he had never heard of England, 'Where is your country, then?'

There was a moment while Ceri wondered whether to trust him. Then she said, 'It's under the sea.'

His eyes widened for a moment at that; eyes like the sea, Ceri thought, blue or grey as the light caught them. But he didn't laugh. All he said was, 'Tell me about it.'

'It's green,' she said, 'like the sea, and the sky is silver. When the wind is right – we call it the current, but they call it the wind – you can hear the whales singing.'

She saw him fold his hands, very deliberately, his thumbs side by side, mirroring each other.

'What songs do the whales sing?' he asked. As if he were

really interested. And still he wasn't smiling at her, the way grown-ups did when they were humouring her; she had caught a glimpse of it even in Ruth's face last night. Ceri took a deep breath.

'Secret songs,' she answered.

'And these people, who call the current the wind – who are they?'

'I don't know yet.'

Euan said, 'Haven't you decided?'

'No!' she said. 'It's not like that. I haven't found out. All I know is . . . they never say anything they don't mean, and they never say anything unless they have to. Except when they're singing, and then it doesn't matter.'

'I'd like to go there,' he said.

'So'd I, sometimes. There's always something to drag you back.' Ceri threw another pebble across the beach: it skittered over the stones. 'Where do you— ?' she began, but the last words crumbled into a mistake between the back of her throat and her lips, the way words so often did if she tried to say them too fast. 'Did I get that very wrong?'

'Fairly,' Euan said, in an even voice, as if he were neither amused or puzzled, the way so many people would have been.

Ceri sighed. 'Mum used to jump on me like a trampoline if I made mistakes. Now she just lets me make them.' She looked at him. 'Is it wort – wor – oh, what *is* the sound?'

'Th?' Euan suggested.

'Th,' said Ceri, and then, 'Worth. Were you ever a speech therapist?'

He laughed. 'You don't sound as if you liked the idea.'

'I was plagued with them once.' Ceri didn't add, after I was ill. 'I hated them. Always just sounds, no words. Baa baa black sheep. Baa baa baa.' She stopped short. I'm telling him all these things, and I never even told Mum before.

'So how would you have learnt the sound of b?' Euan asked.

'Brightest and best of the sons of the morning,' Ceri said promptly. Why does nobody else ask me this sort of question?

'Mm,' Euan said. 'Word magic.'

'I like that. Tell me more.'

'I think you know all I could tell you.'

'Don't know what you mean,' Ceri said.

He turned his head and looked at her again. 'But what were you going to ask? Is it worth . . . ?'

'Only, was it worth repeating the question?'

'Depends how important the answer is,' he said, a smile lifting the corners of his mouth. 'And whether you'll get one.'

'Well – where do you come from, then?'

'Ah,' Euan said, unlacing his fingers. Ceri was still waiting for his answer, when she saw the seal again. Its head first, sleek and round, two dark eyes staring at them from a face that looked surprisingly human. Then it rolled sideways on the surface of the water, like a cat on a sunlit pavement, and floated there with one flipper up. Ceri looked from the seal to Euan, to see if he had noticed it; and one of his hands was raised in what looked like greeting.

'Suppose you must see them all the time,' Ceri said.

'Yes.'

'We hardly ever go places by the sea,' Ceri said. 'I've never been so close to a seal.'

'I could get you closer, if you like,' said Euan. Not as if he were boasting, but matter-of-factly. When Ceri looked at him he was gazing out across the water. The seal dived noiselessly, hardly a swirl in the water; and Euan smiled. It seemed to Ceri for a moment as if she could feel every drop of her blood alive inside her. She said, 'I would like – but – who are you, anyway? I don't know you at all.' Suddenly her heart started thumping wildly. How much had she told this stranger? What would he be thinking of her? Ceri shifted uneasily.

He said, 'But I think I know who you are . . . though Ruth seemed to think you might not talk to me, when I saw her earlier.'

'Oh!' Ceri said. 'Are you Ruth's – ' she swallowed the phrase she had read in Mum's letter. 'I mean, Ruth's friend?'

'Am I Ruth's what?' he asked with a glint in his eye. 'Don't worry: I can take it.'

'Latest acquisition,' Ceri said. Euan laughed. 'I've had worse thrown at me. But yes, I am.'

There was a silence. Ceri wondered if her cheeks looked as hot as they felt. I suppose I should have guessed, but then how was I to know? He must think I'm so stupid.

'I've taken Ruth out to see the seals before now,' Euan said. 'You're welcome to come, if you don't mind the boat.' The only boat Ceri could think of was the motor-cruiser Mum and Michael had hired once, cruising in the Norfolk Broads. 'Won't it scare them away?'

He shook his head. 'Not the dinghy. Besides – they know me.' There was an odd look to Euan's face as he said this; as if he too heard noises in the wind, songs on the flowing tide. As if his mind was definitely elsewhere. For a moment Ceri stared at him uncertainly. 'You don't really want to,' she said.

'What gave you that idea? I meant it. You are invited.'

'To the seal party. I accept.' Ceri grinned.

'This evening?' Euan asked.

'Wow. If I fix it with Mum.' She scrambled to her feet. Euan stayed where he was. 'If you see Ruth,' he said.

'What?'

'Give her my love.'

I'd almost forgotten already, Ceri thought to herself. I thought he liked talking to me because I was me, not because of Ruth . . . and how am I supposed to tell her what he just said?

But Ruth might have been on another island for all Ceri saw or heard of her for the rest of the day. Mum didn't come back from her walk till lunch, by which time Sam had cooked rabbit stew with not too much help from John MacInnes, and Ceri was so ravenous that she'd eaten hers before she remembered it had been hopping around that morning.

While she and Mum washed up – Sam was excused, having cook's right to relax after the meal – Ceri said, 'I'm going out with Euan in his boat tonight.'

'Who?' Mum said, and Ceri giggled inside. I've a good mind to carry on with the rest of the conversation, so that she knows what it feels like when she does it to me.

'Euan,' she said. 'Ruth's friend.'

'Are you indeed?' Mum said. 'And how did you meet Euan?'

'He turned up on the beach. Ruth must have told him who I was. And he's taking me to see the seals.' Ceri attacked the casserole dish ferociously with the scourer. So don't try to stop me, she said inside her head.

'I hope he can manage a boat. You'd look pretty silly in the water.'

'I can swim!'

'With a thousand pounds' worth of hearing aid in each ear. Hm.' But Mum actually looked a bit amused, which was a good sign. Later in the afternoon she went over to talk to the MacInneses, and came back saying that Euan was reported to be safe as houses on, in or under the water.

'So I can go?'

Mum smiled. 'Words to that effect. But mind you wrap up. It'll be colder than you think.'

Ceri had hoped that she would be let to go out alone: instead they were all three waiting for Euan on the grassy slope outside the house. At last the dinghy nosed out from behind the headland, its reflection on the glassy water shaken by the ripples from the oars. Euan seemed to be rowing completely without effort, the curve of his back flexing with an easy movement as if he were swimming. The oars rose and dipped without a sound, though Ceri couldn't tell whether they really were silent or whether her ears silenced them.

Sam said, 'I thought he would go faster. Boring.'

'You want the Boat Race, you do,' Mum said affectionately.

'He go faster if he tried,' Ceri said, knowing she had meant to say 'He'd go', and wondering whether her mother had heard the mistake. She made no sign of it, and only said, 'Sure you'll be warm enough?'

'Yes, Mum.' Ceri tried not to sound long-suffering, but a frown twitched on Mum's forehead all the same. They crunched down the beach just as the dinghy ran out of depth: Euan climbed out in two easy strides and hauled it farther up. 'Evening,' he said. 'Anyone else coming?'

'Only me,' Ceri said, crossing her fingers and holding her

29

breath: though it obviously wasn't Sam's sort of thing. He was ostentatiously hopping up and down, flapping his arms to keep warm, but Euan was barefoot and in shorts. Ceri felt over-dressed in her woolly jumper. Euan must have caught her looking at him, for he said, 'I never get cold. Here, you'd better put this on. Buoyancy aid.' He helped her on with it over her head, and clicked the straps.

'Not that you're going to fall in,' Mum said dubiously. Ceri took the aids from her ears and held them out. 'If you're so sure I will, you better take care of these.'

'You *won't* fall in,' Mum said. The movement of her lips and the sounds Ceri heard slotted in like jigsaw pieces. 'And you won't hear a word Euan says.'

'I hear Euan,' Ceri answered, and Euan said, 'I'll not need to say much.' His words seemed to fly to Ceri's ears and land there, precise as homing birds. She was still holding out the aids. Take them, she willed. Take them.

In the end Mum shrugged and picked the aids out of Ceri's palm. 'I suppose safe is better than sorry.'

I won, Ceri exulted silently, and said aloud, 'I can manage,' as Euan offered to help her into the dinghy. Euan towed it afloat, climbed in as easily as he had got out, and swung the dinghy round with one oar. He looked over his shoulder, pulled on the other oar, and began rowing a straight course. Ceri kept her hand on the side of the boat. Only a plank of wood between her and deep water. There was a smell of damp wood – was it wood? maybe it was seaweed, or salt. Already her hands felt cold on the clammy varnish. The wind wasn't very strong, but it seemed to find its way up her sleeves and down her neck; and her hair, pushed out of place by the buoyancy aid, tickled her ears. Ceri looked briefly over the side: white sand and black rock, under water like green glass. She lifted her hand and licked salt from her fingers.

'How deep?'

'Five fathoms. Thirty feet.'

Ceri hurriedly translated feet into metres. Nine, about. 'Already?'

'Drops very sharply here.' Euan looked over his shoulder again. 'See that gap ahead of us?'

'Water between two lands?'

'That's the one. Point at it, then I can steer straight.'

Mum was right: it was cold out on the water. Ceri stuck one finger out of the sleeve of her jumper, and watched the gap ahead, and the way the light moved on Euan's skin. She wondered if the boat made a noise as it moved through the water. With the hand that was flat on the woodwork she could feel each stroke of the oars as Euan rowed.

At last they were through the gap. 'Loch Teacuis,' Euan said, and spelt it out for her.

The evening was very still. Even the water was hardly moving, and then with big, slow ripples as if it was thick and creamy. 'Tide's on the turn,' said Euan as they slid past a small islet, brown rock, white barnacles, black seaweed, all reflected in reverse until Ceri couldn't tell at which line the water started. Euan was rowing very carefully now, with tiny strokes, sometimes lifting the oars clear of the water and letting the dinghy drift. Ceri's ears were pinging faintly: she tried to line the noise up with the droplets that slid to the end of the oars and fell ringing into the water.

Suddenly Euan leaned forward and pointed, not sticking his

arm out but keeping his hand close to his chest. Ceri followed the line of his pointing finger. There on the edge of another island was something that at first looked as if it had been washed up accidentally.

Euan shipped the oars altogether, laying them in the bottom of the dinghy, and clouting one of her ankles with a blade as he did so. Ceri hardly noticed, for the thing on the island was moving: it was a seal.

They drifted closer. What Ceri had thought were long rounded boulders turned out to be other seals, lifting their heads, blinking, and settling back as if they had seen all they wanted and didn't think much of it.

'Will they come here?' she said.

'I'll try. Sit very still.' Euan stood up in the middle of the boat, drew a deep breath, and began to sing. There were no words, only music: she heard it very clearly. The seals lifted their heads again. Then slowly they shuffled to the water's edge, plopped in, and disappeared.

'Ohh,' Ceri said: then all at once the seals were round the boat, crowding it, but never bumping against it.

'Can I lean over?'

'Kneel in the bilges first.' Euan sat down again.

'The what?'

Euan indicated the water on the bottom boards.

'Are we leaking?'

He laughed, and shook his head. 'Not particularly. All boats have bilgewater. You can hold onto the gunwale – the edge.'

'Ugh.' But Ceri could see that she would be safest in the middle of the boat, so she knelt down. Almost at once a seal bobbed out of the water and looked her straight in the eye. Ceri looked aside at Euan, wanting, but hardly daring, to ask if she could touch it. As if he had heard her thought, he reached out his own hand and stroked the seal's head.

'Me too?' Ceri asked, and he nodded: so she leaned a little farther, and stretched out her arm.

She had expected the seal to be cold and wet. But it was warm, warm as if there was a fire stoked inside it, and soft. She let her hand rest there. 'Lovely to swim with them,' she said.

'I have.'

'Have you?' Ceri looked at Euan. He was staring at the seals as hard as she had been, and there was that look in his eyes she had noticed in the morning. Tentatively, not quite sure how he would answer, she drew in her breath for a question. 'Would you?' she asked. 'Now?'

Euan grinned at her, put both hands on the bow, and vaulted neatly into the water. Ceri crouched down, steadying herself against the rocking boat, and watched him. He swam exuberantly, like no one she had ever seen before, diving and rolling and twisting. In the water the seals themselves were no longer awkward oval rocks, but sleek and slim, pouring themselves like other streams of grey water through the waves. It was difficult to tell, among the wet glinting curves of skin and body, what was seal and what was Euan.

When at last the seals swam away again, Euan surfaced laughing, and shook the wet hair back from his face. For a moment Ceri thought she saw a line like a scar on his scalp, but she couldn't be sure.

'How you getting in again?' she asked, her tongue stumbling among the words.

'With difficulty.' He pointed. 'You sit there, on the stern

33

thwart. Port side. Left. I'll climb in starboard.'

Ceri scrambled back and sat at the stern, feeling the dinghy rock alarmingly even under only her own weight. Euan put his hands on the gunwale at the starboard bow, heaved, and stayed half in and half out for a moment before tipping into the dinghy with an awkward tangle of arms and legs. He sat up, smiled, and said, 'Don't try this at home.'

'Swimming's easier.'

'*Yes*,' he said. There was a strange vehemence in his voice that Ceri could not understand. He picked up the oars and began to row towards the shore. The nearby hillside was dappled green and brown and purple under the evening sun. A movement caught Ceri's eye.

'There's Ruth.'

Euan looked round, startled, and his mouth moved fiercely. Ruth was careering down the hill like a fox in front of hounds, her red hair flaming. Euan pressed his lips together and bent his back to the rowing, so that the dinghy pushed forward at the point of a v-shaped wave that spread across the loch, disturbing the reflections.

Ruth was already knee-deep in the water when they reached the shore. Her face was white, so white that Ceri could see the blue veins in her temples.

'Euan!' Ruth cried, so loudly that her voice reached Ceri's ears as clearly as his. 'You promised you wouldn't! You promised!' She pulled him out of the boat and on to dry land, leaving Ceri to make her way ashore on her own, or stay where she was. Ceri stood up, hesitated, then decided to stay in the dinghy. When she looked at Ruth and Euan again, they were standing close together, anger crackling between them like a thunderstorm.

Four

Euan said, 'And when did I ever promise?'

Ruth stared at him. Ceri had opened her mouth to say hallo, but now her mouth was hijacked by questions. What's going on? What promises?

'You did. You know you did.' Ruth's fingers were digging into his bare arms, making white bloodless hollows in his skin. Euan reached up, pulled her hands away and said, 'I've made no promises yet. We'll talk later. I have to take Ceri back.'

Ruth looked towards the boat as if she noticed Ceri for the first time. 'Oh. Ceri. Hi.' She made one step forward, and Ceri saw that she was barefoot.

'Hi,' Ceri said, and nothing more, because she was so obviously not going to get an answer to any of the questions.

Euan climbed back into the dinghy; it rocked slightly, grating on the pebbles, and Ceri clutched at the gunwale. Ruth, intent and expressionless, watched Euan. Then she waded into the water again and held out her hand to Ceri. 'Why not come back to my place? You can walk to the MacInneses' farm easy from there.'

'We rowed a long way,' Ceri said, looking at Euan, then up at the dappled autumn-coloured slope of the hill. I hope Ruth doesn't think I mean she lied to me, she thought with a sudden flash of nervousness.

'Almost in a circle,' said Euan; and then softly, but still audibly, and as if he could read what she was thinking, 'I won't mind.'

Maybe it was that, being given her own choice, that made Ceri say, 'I'll go back in the boat.'

Ruth shrugged. 'Whatever you like. But come and see me one day.' She shoved the dinghy off, and Euan took one hand from the oar for as long as it took to touch her arm. Ruth looked at him: they did not speak, but something crackled in the air again. Ruth leaned forward, kissed Euan briefly on the lips, and began to walk up the sloping beach.

For a moment Ceri hardly knew where to look. They had kissed each other as if she wasn't there, and she could almost feel the crackle of their contact on her own lips. And what did it really feel like? Her gaze rested on Euan's mouth, and slipped aside. Euan, face to the shore as he rowed away, seemed to be watching Ruth; Ceri looked steadily out to sea. When they were out of the loch and on open water, she said, 'Stop.'

Euan performed a complicated manoeuvre with the oars, and the dinghy stayed where it was, rocking slightly. The ripples were smaller and faster now, and there was a breeze blowing. 'Anything wrong?' he asked.

'No. No. I wanted to . . .' Ceri struggled for words, 'to feel what it was like. I was never on the sea before.' But that wasn't everything. She felt as if she needed time to breathe; as if the small crackling storm that hovered over Ruth and Euan might strike her as well. Give the air a chance to clear, she thought.

Euan laid the oars in the bottom of the boat. 'Do you like it?'

'It's quiet.'

'Aren't things always quiet?' he said.

'I'm not *that* deaf. And anyway I get noise in my head most of the time. Tinnitus. Hissing.'

'I apologise.'

Ceri smiled at him. 'You don't need to. Nobody else does.'

Euan laughed gently, and Ceri was reminded of the first time she had seen him smile. So why did you really ask him to stop? she asked herself.

To look at the sea.

Don't try and get round me; you just wanted to see him smile again.

So?

When he's Ruth's boyfriend?

She tried to stop thinking before the next answer arrived, and hugged her arms around herself. 'Euan,' she said.

'What?'

'Oh, nothing.' But that sounded too stupid, so she asked, 'Why was Ruth in such a – what was the matter?'

Euan said, 'She's afraid of the sea. She needn't be. There's nothing to fear, not for her, not when I'm here.'

Ceri wanted to ask what he meant by that, but when she looked at Euan again he was staring out towards the horizon. They sat in silence for a while. Ceri heard Euan humming under his breath, and then singing. The dinghy had swung round in the wind or tide or current, and Euan was looking westward to the open sea. Under the setting sun a line of light was sparkling on the water.

'He came one night to her bed-foot,

   And a grimly guest I'm sure was he,

Saying, "Here am I, thy bairn's father,

   Although I be not comely".'

Euan went on singing, and the words drifted in and out of Ceri's hearing. It was the tune she had heard at the ceilidh, fading into the noise of the wind. Ceri stared into the water. Beyond the sky's reflection she could see shapes, tenuous and shifting as the tunes she heard in the noise of the car's engine.

Suddenly she realised Euan had stopped singing. 'What do you see?' he asked. 'Round towers of other days in the seas beneath you shining?'

She looked at him. 'Did you make that up?'

'No, it's a quotation.'

'I don't know enough *words*,' Ceri said, almost shouting. 'How am I supposed to tell people things? You said exactly what I was trying to think, and I can't even paint it well enough either.' She turned towards him fiercely and said, 'Tell me some more. More about the sea.'

For a moment she thought he was going to shake his head and pick up the oars again; but then he said, 'The dragon-green, the luminous, the dark, the serpent-haunted sea.'

'Mmm.' Ceri closed her eyes. Shapes swirled behind her eyelids. She said, 'That song you were singing. What was it?'

'It's usually called "The Great Silkie of Sule Skerry".'

Ceri opened her eyes, blinking, to the red light of sunset. 'What's a silkie?'

'One of the seal folk.'

'You mean, a seal?'

'More than that,' Euan said, sounding oddly reluctant. 'Half seal and half human – the stories say. They could take their seal skin off and come ashore.'

'Oh.' Ceri could think of nothing more to say. She would have liked to look at Euan; but what would he think? Instead she turned her head aside and looked at the light on the water.

'Shall we go?' Euan said after a while.

'Suppose we must,' she said.

Euan turned the dinghy and rowed on slowly, changing course to bring them ashore where they had set out. The light of the sun was across his face as he nudged the dinghy cautiously against the beach, broadside on. Ceri felt the bottom-boards quiver beneath her feet.

'Coming indoors?' she asked.

He looked up quickly at that, shaking his head. 'No, but thanks.'

The threads of the argument she'd had with herself in the dinghy ravelled through her mind again. Ceri cut them short, drew in a quick breath and put her hands on his where they gripped the oars. 'Will I see you again?'

Now listen what you've done. He'll laugh for sure.

Euan looked either surprised or amused – she couldn't quite tell which. 'Of course.' He looked over the side. 'Can you get out on your own?'

'Watch me.' Ceri shook the sleeves of the woolly jumper back from her hands and gripped the gunwale. Her two steps out weren't as effortless as Euan's, but she couldn't have looked too ungainly. Euan said, 'Goodbye, Ceri,' backed water, and rowed away. Ceri stood there, watching until the boat disappeared round the headland. Once she waved. Euan, both hands full, maybe couldn't be bothered to wave back.

That night Ceri couldn't sleep. She kept thinking of Ruth. And Euan. I wish I'd known who Euan was when he first arrived. Then I wouldn't have – admit it, Ceri – wouldn't have found him so interesting. She opened her eyes into the dark. Has Ruth changed? We seem different together. Or am I just imagining things? Maybe it's me that's changed.

After lying in bed for what felt like hours, she switched on the light, knelt up and rummaged through the shelf of stray books for anything worth reading. There was a book of Scottish folk tales; that would be better than nothing. She lay like an old-fashioned movie star with one foot on the floor, alert for the vibration that might mean Mum was moving around and would see the light under the door.

Some of the stories were full of unpronounceable Celtic names, and she skipped those; but here and there something caught her eye as she built her house of words to live in the undersea land.

'He saw the stars of the north and the stars of the south and the stars that are under the sea.'

Ceri laid the book quietly on the floor, rolled over, and switched off the light.

The stars that are under the sea.

She went to the window, knelt down, and drew one curtain back. The sky was flooded with moonlight and stars. Blurred gleams of light marked the waves moving on the water. Into her memory drifted the sound of Euan's laughter as he moved swiftly and easily among the seals. She remembered the seal that had risen out of the water and looked at her from its round dark eyes. If only she had thought of it, if only she'd had the courage to jump in the water then, she might have swum with the seals herself.

And then Ceri laughed inside her head at the thought of herself, woolly jumper, buoyancy aid, gumboots and all, in the water. She hardly belonged to her own imaginary country. Yet – the seals did: were they the people who heard the whales singing?

She held her breath. This was like a discovery, not like an invention. It felt right. Ceri trod carefully back towards bed. She found a pencil and her sketch-pad by touch, and wrote in the dark on the back cover, Go swimming with Euan?

Her pencil stopped before the dot of the question mark. Euan, who swam with the seals. She had asked him where he came from, and he hadn't answered. No, that wasn't quite right. The seal had risen up out of the water and interrupted them. As Ceri rolled over and slid into sleep she could almost hear Euan's voice singing in her ears.

When she came down to breakfast the next morning Mum waved a folded piece of paper at her across the cornflake packet. 'Ruth came by on her way to the ferry. You have an invitation to tea.'

'Do Americans drink tea?' Ceri said, but the unfolded note in front of her read, among other things, 'If Ceri likes to come to tea this afternoon about half after four she'll be welcome.'

'Looks like it,' Mum said. 'Will you go?'

'Why not?' Ceri looked at her mother. 'Don't you want me to?' she asked, not sure what had given her that idea: something in the angle of her mother's head, perhaps.

Mum's hand went up to her lips in the gesture she had unconsciously retained from the time when she smoked, and Ceri knew that she was on edge. Whatever Mum said was behind her hand.

41

'I didn't hear you,' Ceri said.

Mum looked at her fingers as if she didn't recognise them, clenched her hands in each other, and said, 'I don't mind. Ruth is her mother's daughter more than her father's, thank goodness.'

Ceri picked her coffee up and stirred it carefully, although she didn't take sugar. 'What about me?' she asked.

Mum laughed. 'I never knew two people less alike than you and me,' she said. 'But that has nothing to say to anything. What are you planning today? I told Sam I'd take him to Oban, so come if you want to.'

Ceri looked at her for a moment. 'You and me wasn't exactly what I meant,' she said.

Her mother looked back. 'I thought not. But I'm . . . really not prepared to talk about it, if you don't mind.'

Ceri blinked at her, wondering how much further she could push it. Mum was never at her best at breakfast. And she wasn't sure she had the energy herself. She sighed, and took the easy option. Anything for a quiet life. 'I'll just laze, today,' she said, 'thanks. But you better tell me how to get to Ruth's.'

'Oh, I'll show you,' Mum said over her shoulder, climbing the stairs and heading along the gallery to the inland door. 'Come up here.'

They went through the open door and across the green lawn where the fence divided the smooth turf from the rough. Mum scrambled up the bank beyond the track, and when she joined her Ceri realised that there was another, lower, hill that had been out of sight from the doorway. Beyond it was a sliver of blue water, and on the slope, surrounded on three sides by slanting thorn trees, was a cottage.

'Think you can find your way there?' Mum said, teasing.

'Of course!' Ceri skidded back down again. 'Don't worry about me.'

Once Mum and Sam left, she meant to paint, or listen to music: but Ceri found herself going out of the seaward door again and down to the water's edge. If this loch was an inlet from the Atlantic, then somewhere on the other side of it, beyond that pale, no-coloured light that seemed to hang around this horizon all day long, was her father. A thousand miles and fifteen years away, a stranger on the far side of her own ignorance.

Will I ever know what I'm missing? He is where half of me came from, after all. Ruth could tell me, I suppose. With the thought of Ruth there came into Ceri's head a tumbled scurry of ideas. After a long moment she realised that they were mostly connected with Euan.

Slowly she picked her way along the shore, heading some-where near where she remembered Euan rowing the dinghy. At the foot of the headland was a tumbled confusion of rocks, with one long outcrop of grey stone stretching into the sea, and waves creaming over it. Ceri sat down and began to watch for seals. If none came, then she would think about the stars that are under the sea. Narrow blades of light cutting through the water.

What she saw, suddenly, although he must have been there all the time, was Euan. He was crouched on the grey outcrop, singing. His back was to her, and yet she could hear his voice, though not the words. She could not see whether he was singing to anyone, or anything; and after a few minutes Euan put his hands together above his head, rocked on the balls of his feet, and dropped into the water with a neat and splashless dive. Ceri stood up: but she could see no more, and eventually turned inland.

There was a narrow road around the edge of the hollow, above Ruth's cottage. It did not go down to the sea, but snaked back inland; Ceri decided it was probably the road they had arrived by on Saturday night. She found a vantage point on the hillside, and sat with the noise of the wind in her ears. How long would she have to wait, how much could she think about – or avoid thinking about? With an effort she wrenched her thoughts round to her undersea country. At night, with strange creatures moving like moonlit ghosts through the water.

At last she saw Ruth coming home, and ran down to join her at the gate.

'Hallo, sis,' Ruth said, and it sounded like a word in a strange language. Ceri grinned. 'Hallo yourself. Can I do anything?'

'No,' Ruth said, stooping for the post off the door-mat. 'Just give me a moment to clear, and I'll be right with you.'

Ceri wandered across the room, stroking a piece of pottery that was smooth as slow-running water, fingering a shawl that lay like a woolly rainbow across the back of a chair.

'I saw this odd thing,' she said.

'Tell,' Ruth said, stacking the papers on her desk square to its corners.

'Euan, sitting on a rock, singing.'

'Oh.' Ruth's voice was flatly indifferent; but then she burst out, 'I wish he wouldn't!'

'Why shouldn't he?' Ceri said. 'If I could sing I'd sing to the sea.'

'That's different.'

How? why? Ceri wanted to ask, but thought better of it. She watched as Ruth picked a thin blue letter from the pile on the desk, made a face at it, and ripped it open; and then sensed not silence so much as stillness: she could see Ruth's back and neck stiffen, as if she was about to lose her temper. Ruth seemed to take a long time reading; but when she turned round the letter was a tiny blue square in her hands, folded as small as she could get it. She hurled the pellet into the waste-paper basket, stamped once, and said, 'You want a drink?'

'You said tea.'

'I sure did. And I need some hot tea. They say it's good for shock.' Ruth went into the kitchen as if she was looking for something to throw. When the phone rang she came storming back, snatched up the receiver, and shouted, 'Yes?'

There was a pause.

'Euan!' Ruth said. 'I thought you – oh, sure thing . . .' The conversation went on, like trying to read a sentence with half of each letter missing. 'But sure you can – only, Euan, my father just wrote me . . . don't *laugh*, he's coming here – no I can not, he's on the plane right now.' A long pause, while Ruth listened intently, stroking the receiver where it lay against her face. 'I guess you're right,' she said at last. 'Uh-huh.' And she added something Ceri couldn't hear, while a smile wrapped itself round her lips.

Ruth laid the receiver down gently, and went back for the tea. She gave one mug to Ceri, and stood cradling the other against herself as if her heart was cold. 'Some tea party,' she said. 'I knew I should have let the mail wait. Did you hear me?'

'Mostly,' Ceri said.

'I had an air-mail from my father.'

'He's my father too.' And he was coming to Scotland, but Ruth hadn't exactly mentioned that.

'I know, I know.' Ruth took a sip of tea and looked at Ceri

over the rim of the mug. 'You are so like him.'

'But what's he *like*?' Ceri asked.

Ruth smiled uncomfortably. 'Tall dark handsome stranger. All my girl friends go wild over him. But I don't see him that much. He can be – difficult.' She walked across the room and looked out of the window, still hugging the warm drink to her. 'I liked having your mom around. I was only a kid, but I could see she made him . . . more fun to stay with. And you were a cute baby!'

Ceri ignored the last bit. 'Why did she go?'

'Didn't she tell you?'

'She never tells me anything,' Ceri said. 'Did you say – he's coming here?' She supposed she ought to be more excited; but sheer curiosity was all that seemed to be driving her at the moment.

'Yes.' Ruth looked at her. 'Did you meet him before?'

'Not to remember. I was three.' Ceri paused. 'I want to.'

Ruth said slowly, 'If your mom won't tell, then I guess maybe I shouldn't . . . you have to remember, they divorced. And it wasn't just pretty please may I go home.'

I suppose I ought to have known that much. Ceri looked down into her mug of tea. She said, 'What about you? And him?'

Ruth drew a deep breath and said, 'He likes the idea of me for a daughter. I look good and he can take me about. I went along with that for a while, but being his daughter left no room for the real me.' She swallowed down some tea, and turned away briskly as if to stop Ceri asking any more questions; but remembered to turn back again and face her when she asked, 'Cake? I'll get this tea party together if it kills me.'

46

'Yes, please,' Ceri said, biting back her frustration. *I was so near to finding out more. But anyway – now I know for sure, he looks like me.*

Ruth was a long time in the kitchen. Ceri stood drinking her tea. *I suppose I could sit down.* Instead she went slowly through the other door; into the bedroom.

It was a double bed. Neat and tidy, but still: double.

And Ruth isn't married.

Well, a lot of people aren't, these days.

Do you suppose she – well –

Anything to stop herself thinking about it. Ceri sat on the end of the bed, where it fitted under an arch that looked like a fireplace. In the wall beside it was a small iron-hinged door with an old black latch; but the padlock that locked it was new and shiny-bright. Ceri put her hand on the wood, and felt a cold draught round the edge of the door. It must lead up into the chimney. The walls were stone, and thick; the wind outside would not shake them, nor would movement indoors. Whatever was locked in that cupboard was out of reach of the world, as safe from it as a child not yet born; and yet in that cold sharp draught on her hand, like starlight under the sea, Ceri felt it calling to her.

Five

Ceri turned round to see Ruth standing in the doorway with a plate of cake. 'Want some?' Ruth asked.

Ceri swallowed the last mouthful of tea. 'Please.' Back in the other room, she asked, 'What do you keep in that cupboard by the bed?'

Ruth looked at her. 'How do you know I keep anything?'

'It's locked.'

Ruth laughed. 'I keep secrets, then.' Her glance slid aside, and Ceri, following her gaze, saw two small keys lying on a corner of the desk. Ignore them. She looked the other way, into the kitchen, and said, though she already knew the answer, 'Was that Euan who phoned?'

'Yes,' Ruth said.

Will she mind if I ask? I do know he's her boyfriend, I saw it in Mum's letter, except of course I'm not supposed to know that. And has Euan told her what I called him – latest acquisition? Ceri felt her head buzzing.

'Are you – you and he – ?' And then she stopped. Do sisters ask each other this kind of question?

'Yes,' Ruth said again. 'We are.' She smiled, but not at Ceri.

Ceri nodded. 'I've never had a boyfriend.'

'Oh, your time will come.'

'Supposing it already came, and I missed it?'

'You don't miss something like that,' Ruth said. Ceri looked at her, tall and self-assured, her hair like a glowing flame. It's easy for you to say that. You've got Euan. Suppose you try being me for a change, missing even the obvious things because I was looking the wrong way. Ceri bit her lip. I'm jealous. This is disgusting. She refused to think what exactly she was jealous of.

Ruth lifted her head. 'Someone at the door. Come in!' she called, and a moment later Fergal who had danced with her at the ceilidh walked in, his fair hair ruffled and the skin on his nose sunburn-pink round the freckles. He saw Ceri, stopped, and said, 'Oh, hi,' and clicked his fingers twice. 'Ceri. Ceri Hughes.'

'Ceri Schaefer,' Ceri said.

'My mistake.' Fergal grinned. 'Am I allowed to be friendly? We met at the ceilidh.'

'I remember.'

'How could she not?' Ruth said, and she and Fergal went into a quick fire of jokes and retorts of which Ceri caught about one word in ten. Suddenly Ruth caught her eye, said, 'Sorry. I forgot.' Fergal looked mystified; neither Ruth nor Ceri explained, and slowly the afternoon changed into something like a real tea party. Except that once Fergal said, 'Hey, Ruth – Euan's been looking all along the loch shore for something, he won't say what. Did he tell you? Do you know?'

'No. He did not,' Ruth said, too quickly. 'Another cake, sis?'

Ceri shook her head, watching Ruth's gaze slip sideways to the desk where the two keys lay. Fergal glanced that way, and then back at Ceri. His grey eyes were disconcertingly direct. She looked away from him, and found herself staring through the open door of the room at the locked cupboard in the wall. Fergal got up for some more cake, which meant coming to stand beside her; and she saw his gaze flick across where she had been looking.

When he sat down again he crumbled the piece of cake on his plate and ate the bits separately, masking whatever he might have been saying with his fingers: and after a little while he looked accusingly at Ceri.

'You're not laughing,' he said to her.

'I can't hear you.' After a second she added, 'Not properly. I lip-read.'

Fergal looked truly disconcerted for a moment; then he shrugged it off and laughed. 'You've not missed much. Shall I walk you back? I've some eggs to collect from Aunt Morag.'

'If you like.' Ceri smiled at Ruth. 'I enjoyed your tea party.'

'Mad Hatter's tea party,' Ruth said inconsequentially. 'My best to your mom.'

Ceri went outside while Fergal said goodbye; he joined her by the gate, and they walked up the slope in silence.

'What's that behind your ear?' Fergal asked suddenly, turning to look at her. 'And – er – do you mind my asking?'

'No. I told you I lip-read, so what does it look like?' Ceri said, taking a big step up on to a boulder and wobbling dangerously before she got her balance again.

'Okay, okay, so it's a deaf aid,' Fergal said, stepping up beside her. 'Keep your hair on.'

Ceri tucked a smile into the corners of her mouth. 'It's not an aid to deaf. It's an aid to hearing.'

'I get you. It helps you hear.'

'Sometimes,' Ceri said. 'But mostly it helps the hearing. They think they needn't speak up.' She jumped down from the boulder on to a patch of grass, and heard what she guessed must be a brief explosion of laughter from Fergal. It was hard to tell without looking at him. A moment later he tapped her on the shoulder, and when she turned round, said, 'Come this way. There's a grand view from the top.'

They sat down, the wind flapping giant invisible sheets against them. Fergal said something.

'Try again,' Ceri said. 'Too loud up here.'

Fergal laughed again. 'Have you always been deaf?'

'I'm not deaf.'

He shrugged. 'Okay. So what are you, and have you always been it?'

'I'm hard of hearing. That's what they call it.' Ceri thought for a moment. 'I could hear – normally, or whatever you like to say, before I was ill. But I can't remember much about that. It was like a black hole, it swallowed everything.' First Euan and now Fergal. Why is it so much easier, talking to strangers?

Fergal looked at her. 'I've never been very ill. Were you near dying?' He looked uncomfortable talking about illness and death at the top of his voice; as if he had been caught shouting in church.

'I suppose so,' Ceri said. 'It was meningitis. I could have been dead. Or completely deaf. Or blind.' She blinked, and looked around. 'I'm glad I wasn't.'

'Do you hate it?'

'Well . . . how can I? It's – normal, for me. What I hate is other people, when they can't be bothered. They mumble. And they spend ages trying to tell me things I don't need to know. And when I do want to know they say it doesn't matter.'

'I bet you get angry.'

Ceri glanced at him; he was looking quite sympathetic. 'I want to scream and shout and howl,' she said. 'But what's the good?'

He laughed. 'At least they'd know you were there.'

'They'd only tell me not to make a fuss and remember there are lots of people worse off.'

'And so there are.'

'But that doesn't help *me*,' Ceri said. The wind billowed again, and she said, 'It really is noisy up here. In my hearing aids. Couldn't we go down?'

'Och, sure,' Fergal said, and began walking downhill.

Even through the rough air Ceri heard the accent, and said, 'You don't always talk like that.'

'Like what?'

'Scotch.'

'Scotch is whisky. I'm Scottish,' Fergal said, his voice coming through clearly as the slope dipped into a sheltered hollow. 'And I do, you know.'

'You mean I don't always hear you.'

'Well—' He hesitated. 'I suppose I do mean that.'

'Then say so.'

Fergal looked at her. 'We can't all remember to be perfect for you, woman.'

'*Oh*—' Ceri hovered between losing her temper, and ignoring him. A couple of deep breaths. 'Some of you have more to remember than others.' She was relieved when Fergal laughed.

He was only briefly in the farmhouse, and came out cradling a tray of eggs. 'Beware omelettes,' he said grinning. 'See you again.'

Ceri said, awkwardly, 'Thanks for seeing me back. I don't mean to sound the way I do. If I sound mad at you.'

'I know that,' Fergal said, though whether he had known was more than she could say. 'Anyway, I like it.'

Before she could ask what he meant he was gone, walking with the long easy strides of someone used to this rough footing. Ceri picked her way round the yard, walked up the slope to the inland door and stood for a moment on the threshold. No faint throb in the air, no Sam at his stereo; no smell of coffee, no Mum? Ceri walked across the landing. Her mother's bedroom door was open, the double bed looking odd with only one side rumpled. The window was open, and there was a scatter of papers on the floor, including the now-familiar air mail blue. For a moment Ceri hesitated. Then she stepped forward and picked the letter up. It was the one from her mother that she had seen before, about Ruth, still not posted. Slowly she turned it over. Mum had put no address at the top. It began, 'Paul.' Not 'Dear Paul'.

'*Ceri*!'

Ceri jumped. Mum stormed up the last few stairs and snatched the letter out of her hands. 'How *dare* you!'

'But it was on the floor,' Ceri said.

'So what? That's not an invitation to read it!' Mum was obviously stoking up for a real row if Ceri didn't tread cautiously; but she said, 'Ruth had a letter from him.'

54

'Did you read that one too?'

'No!' Ceri looked at her mother. Much more of this and I'll think you don't trust me. She took a deep breath, sorted the sounds out inside her mouth and said carefully, 'He wrote to tell Ruth that he's on his way here.'

If Ceri had shot her, Mum might have reacted the same way. Her face went white, and she reached out shakily so that she could lean on the door-frame. 'Oh God. Oh no.'

Ceri swallowed. She couldn't remember ever seeing her mother look like this before. Trying to put things right, she said, 'Perhaps he doesn't know we're here.'

'He does,' her mother said. 'I bet he does. He's the sort that knows what you'll do. He finds your weak spot and kicks you on it. He likes to be in control. She looked down at the letter, that she was still holding, and deliberately tore it across, and across again.

'But you're talking about my father!' Ceri said.

'Well?'

She paused, confused by her own thoughts, bewildered by her mother's anger. 'So why did you marry him if he was like that?'

'Because I was fool enough to love him,' Mum said, tight-lipped.

'But what did he do? Why did you leave him?'

'It's what he is. Not so much what he does. I don't want to talk about him. Ceri, *please*!'

Ceri stared at her mother. Her neat and precise mother, shaking at the knees. And then the phone rang.

Mum stifled a yelp, and went downstairs again. Ceri leaned over the rail and watched her as she walked to the kitchen; a fragment of the letter fell from the stairs and drifted to the floor.

Her mother came out into the hall. 'It's Ruth. Do you want to try with the amplifier?'

'No,' Ceri said. 'Not this time. What does she want?'

'Wait a moment.' Mum came back in a few moments and said, 'She says, there were two keys on the desk. Did you pick one up?'

'No.'

'You're sure?'

'Of course I'm sure!'

'Sorry,' her mother said. 'I didn't mean it like that. But she sounds worried.' She went back into the kitchen, looking worried herself, but not about Ruth or her problems.

All through the rest of the evening Mum wouldn't sit still, but wandered in and out looking for something that wasn't there, feeling in her pockets for phantom cigarettes, ignoring the fact that Sam had his feet on the table and Ceri was lying on the floor painting, with her hearing aids out in clear view on the carpet. At last she slid the glass door open and stood looking out on to the loch. The breeze came in and brushed the back of Ceri's hands. Sam looked up, visibly decided not to complain about the draught, and went out of the room.

'Mum?' Ceri said.

Her mother turned round. 'Yes?'

'Are you all ri—' Ceri stopped the question, feeling how pointless it would sound. 'Is there anything I can do?'

'No. Not really.' Mum smiled. 'Go to bed, love.'

It felt too early for bed: once she had taken her hearing aids out, Ceri put on the enormous t-shirt she wore for wandering round the flat at home early in the mornings, and knelt by her bedroom window. The loch was a dapple of light and dark, a flicker of movement that almost had its own sound. The moon, thinned to a lemon shape now, was rising through a cloudy sky.

Ceri leaned her elbows on the low sill. If only inside was as peaceful as outside. She remembered thinking about people and chemistry, some time . . . if Mum was on the point of some reaction? explosion? – how could she keep clear? It seemed unlikely she could actually do anything to stop the bang.

The dapples on the surface of the loch swirled and shifted in the dark. Mum. Ruth. Her father. Bouncing round like atoms and molecules, Ceri in the middle; and somewhere outside, on the edge, Euan.

She would never have tired of looking at the water; but one of her feet began to go numb. Ceri stood up and rubbed her knees, feeling the roughness of the carpet printed on her skin. There was a movement beneath her in the twilight, a face pale as the fog-hidden moon turned up to hers. Ruth, beckoning.

Quietly Ceri slipped out of the room and down the stairs. A slice of light across the hall meant that Mum was in the kitchen still. Ceri sidled into the lounge. A slap of cold air across her face; the sliding door was still open. She squeezed through the gap and walked towards Ruth.

It was almost impossible for Ceri to hear in the dark, even with her hearing aids, because lip movements were just too indistinct; and of course she'd left the aids behind in the rush to get down here. But Ruth had thought of that. She folded Ceri's hands round a small bundle like an unwieldy cushion, held up a scrap of paper, tucked that into the bundle, and ran off silently before Ceri could so much as draw breath to ask a question.

Not that I would have heard the answer. Ceri stepped into

the house again, stubbed her toe against the track the door slid on, and bit her lip to stop herself crying out. She closed the door and fled upstairs, expecting Mum to come and see what the noise had been, or Sam to look round his half-open door as she crossed the landing; but under her feet the floor remained silent. She wedged her bedroom door shut with the chair cushions, and walked towards the window. The sky had cleared, and the moon was shining in.

Ceri took the bundle more firmly in her two hands and shook it out. It fell glimmering, like moonlight on water, or on wet skin. About as long as she was tall, an odd shape, oval, or leaf-like. Two dark holes at one end. Ceri held the thing up so they looked at her. She had seen those two dark almost-human shapes before, looking up at her out of the water. It was a seal's skin.

She dropped it as if it had burnt her. How could Ruth keep this dead thing? How could she, Ceri, keep it, now that she had seen live seals? Ceri remembered suddenly how she had once touched a sealskin cape at a jumble sale. But . . . she knelt down. This wasn't the same. Something different. Something she couldn't put a name to. She picked the skin up and buried her face in it. The smell: dried salt, a faint tang of seaweed. The smell of the sea. The skin was warm in her hands. Ceri looked at it, turned it over. The piece of paper slipped to the floor, an extra flake of moonlight. Ruth's writing, with its elaborate American capitals.

Now you know what I keep in the cupboard. But not with a key missing. Don't tell anyone.

But who might I tell? And all at once the memories of words came tumbling into Ceri's mind. Fergal, talking of Euan hunting for something along the foreshore. Ruth turning the question aside, too quickly, too soon. And something else, from the evening before.

Ceri crouched there, her tinnitus like an echo of the sound of the sea in her ears, trying to remember. She shut her eyes, and could almost see the moonlight through her closed eyelids. What else was it I heard? What am I trying to remember? And at last the echo came clear.

'Half seal and half human – the stories say.' And that song, that song again.

> 'I am a man upon the land
> And I am a silkie in the sea
> But when I'm far and far from land
> My home it is in Sule Skerry.'

Euan, singing.

Six

It was impossible. Of course it was impossible. There was not the tiniest pinch of real visible proof. Ceri played with the idea, laying out all the things she knew or thought she knew, or guessed, so that they meant nothing. And silently, behind her back almost, while she was trying to disprove them, the pieces built themselves again into a statement of fact: Euan is a silkie, and this is his seal skin.

So, okay, Ceri thought to herself. I'll try believing it. She looked down at the skin where it lay across her lap in the moonlight. Euan's looking for it, if Fergal's right. And if he isn't right, then at least Ruth must think Euan's looking. Or else she wouldn't be worrying, hedging him round with promises. Now if I were in her place – Ceri bit her lip. There it was, right out in the open at last.

Even her thoughts were silent for a while, drifting on the faint white noise that forever hissed like phantom snakes inside her ears.

Would I want to be? Do I want to be? In Ruth's place? She rocked backwards and forwards on her knees, her arms crossed,

61

fingers digging into her shoulders. Imagining Euan. Imagining
– no farther.

He wouldn't look at me.

But he does. He took you to see the seals.

Only being kind to Ruth's kid sister.

But he smiles at you.

He can do that without meaning anything.

You always hear him. That's got to be important.

I suppose it has. Yes, it must be.

You can always play it for pretend. No real blood. It needn't
be that important.

Okay. I pretend. It's a game.

And then Ceri lowered her hands, and felt the seal skin brush
her fingers. What is real, and what isn't – and how to tell?
Clouds billowed outside again, covering the moon completely.
She felt immensely tired. Stumbling, as if she had walked a long
way, she dragged herself to bed, pushing the seal skin down
between the mattress and the wall, to wait for tomorrow.

After breakfast she leaned on the fence between the house and
the MacInneses' farm, watching for movement behind their
kitchen window. Last night's clouds still churned slowly across
the sky, and a sly wind buffeted her from unexpected directions.
She wanted to talk to Fergal, but there were too many
MacInneses in the phone book: and she had no idea when he
would visit his aunt and uncle again . . . maybe if she was clever
she could get Morag MacInnes to pass the message on, and
never have to use the phone herself.

Someone tapped her shoulder, and Ceri jumped, biting short
a yelp.

'Hey!' Sam said in an injured tone. 'Anyone would think I was the Loch Ness monster the way you react.'

'You come creeping up on me – ' Ceri looked at Sam's boots and laughed. 'Okay, clomping up like that, what do you expect?'

'Well, if you will drape yourself round a fence-post and dream,' Sam said. 'What were you doing last night?'

'*What*?' Ceri swallowed. 'I mean, what makes you think I was doing anything?'

'I heard you, of course.'

A flame of irritation lit up inside Ceri's head like a struck match. 'You needn't sound so smug about it.'

Sam flushed, and bit his lip. Then he said, 'Look, Ceri, I can hear, you know. I'm not going to stop using the word just because you don't like it.'

'Shut up,' Ceri said. 'Shut up shut up shut up.'

Sam shrugged. 'Fine.' He turned away, squared his shoulders, and walked back to the house. Ceri's anger went out in a cold splash of guilt. I wonder what he came out for. Did he want to tell me something?

Morag MacInnes came out of the farmhouse and shook out a table-cloth. Ceri waved uncertainly. 'Mrs MacInnes?'

Fergal's aunt walked towards the fence, folding the cloth as she came. 'What can I do for you?' she asked, and tucked a loose strand of hair back behind her ear.

'I wanted to ask Fergal something . . . do you have his telephone number?'

'Och, there's no call for that,' Mrs MacInnes said. 'He'll be here in a bit while, I'll tell him you're wanting to talk with him.'

No need to telephone. A flutter of relief settled in Ceri's

mind. Now all she had to deal with was the rest of the world. Slowly she trailed indoors. On the landing there was a fluorescent sunburst as Sam emerged from the bathroom.

'Sam,' Ceri said in a small voice, but he swept into his room and banged the door. Ceri sat on her own bed and chewed her knuckles. Then she pushed her hand down behind the mattress, near the pillow. Not there. She moved her hand along. There it is. I'm sure I didn't leave it there. Maybe I moved it in my sleep? She pulled the seal skin out and laid it across her knees. Then she stood up and wrapped herself in it. Outside, the cloud was breaking up, the sunshine bursting on to the water with flares and splashes of light. Ceri rubbed her fingers on the soft cloak round her shoulders. I wonder . . . no, I can't. It belongs to Euan. She wriggled inside it, turned her face to rub her cheek on it, and at last, reluctantly, rolled it up again and stowed it behind the head of her bed.

She had lunch with Mum and Sam. Mum was in her vague mood still, Sam was excruciatingly polite, and neither of them seemed to notice that she was trying to get through on their wavelength. In the middle of the washing up there was a noise that even Ceri heard: Sam broke out of his offended silence to say, 'What is *that*?' and Mum looked out of the window. 'It's a car.'

'Nothing that colour is a car,' Sam said with conviction. 'It's a strawberry ice-cream on wheels.'

'It's Fergal,' Ceri said. 'Can I swap the rest of the drying-up? I want to ask him something.' She handed the cloth to Mum without waiting for an answer, and only just heard the 'Yes, but make sure you remember . . .' as she went outside.

Fergal was already talking to his aunt. Ceri heard her say,

' . . . taken a party out from the hotel, sailing,' and then, 'Here's the young lady wants to ask you something.'

'Yourself, is it?' he said. 'I was going to invite you for a drive, any road.'

'In that?' Actually she thought Sam's description of the car was rather good. Maybe it looked more like a blancmange shape than an ice-cream.

He grinned. 'You won't see it when you're inside it.'

'And remember I won't hear a word you say when we're driving.'

'I'll remember.' Fergal waved to Ceri's mother, and must have signalled something or other, and had an answer, because he said, 'That's okay, then. Hop in.'

They drove up the bare grassy slopes that Ceri had grown used to, and over the top of the ridge. Down a winding road into a twisted wood where the trees seemed as ghostly and ancient as the mountains, their trunks grey with lichen, the tunnels between them dark and mysterious. Fergal handled the car casually on the single track, jamming on the brakes when he had to pull into a passing space, lifting one hand in acknowledgement when other drivers let him by. At last he pulled up on a platform of grass above the shore of a loch, not the one Ceri saw beyond her window, but a stiller place with the reflections of pine trees fringing its edges.

'When did you learn to drive?' Ceri asked.

'Oh, I don't know. Bounced around on Dad's farm as soon as I could reach the pedals. Took the test the day after I was seventeen.' Fergal got out of the car, still talking, and Ceri scrambled to get to a place where she could see his lips: but by the time she was out Fergal had stopped talking, and was near the water's

65

edge. He sat down, turned his head, and said, 'I'm taking it to England next year.'

Ceri made a guess at the chain of thought. 'The car?'

'Yes. When I go to university.'

'I would have thought you'd prefer a Scottish university.'

'Oh, I wanted to go to France and do French,' Fergal said, 'to keep up the Auld Alliance. But they wouldn't have me. So I thought I'd do it somewhere as near France as possible. Then if I get bored with England I can jump off the edge and start swimming.' Fergal looked at her. 'This can't have been what you wanted to know.'

'I want to know about seals,' Ceri said.

Fergal grunted. 'Law, biology or folk-tales?'

'Everything.'

'Conservation of Seals Act 1970. Don't touch, injure, handle or otherwise hinder a seal in the pursuit of its duty – i.e. fish,' Fergal said grinning. 'Unless it's taking them out of your nets. Then you can shoot it.'

'That's not fair!'

'The fishermen do have a living to make,' Fergal said mildly. 'Not but what I don't have some family feeling for the seals too.'

'*Family*?' Ceri wasn't quite sure whether to laugh or not.

'Oh, yes.' He looked at her sideways. 'My mother's a MacAlister, and there's a story that one of the MacAlisters fostered a seal once. And *her* mother's name was McCodrum. One of that clan married a seal-woman.'

'Do you believe all that?' Ceri asked, trying to sound as if she was incredulous; the way someone would be who hadn't guessed about Euan.

'Sometimes,' Fergal said. 'When I'm in the mood. It's –

interesting – to live with.' He pulled up a twist of green, rubbed it, and passed it to Ceri. It smelled aromatic between her fingers, sweet and pungent together. 'Half-a-dozen clans say one of their men married a seal-woman,' he said. 'But – in Scotland – only Sule Skerry has the Great Silkie. Where the seal comes for an earthly woman.'

Ceri said, ' "An earthly nourris sits and sings . . ." '

He looked round abruptly. 'You know it?'

'Was at the ceilidh, remember? But I didn't hear all the words.' Ceri waited for a moment, then asked, 'Where is Sule Skerry?'

'Chunk of rock away out north from Cape Wrath. Nobody lives there. Much.'

'You're so mysterious,' Ceri said. 'Hints and secrets.'

'Oh, no,' Fergal said laughing. 'No, not me. I'm nobody particular. You want someone mysterious, you should look at Euan MacMorran.'

'What?'

Fergal looked at her. 'Was I not loud enough?'

'I heard you,' Ceri said. 'But he told me his name was Roane.'

'Did he?' Fergal frowned. 'Strange. I've known him years. He's always been Euan MacMorran to me.'

'What does it mean?'

'Roane?' There was a pause while Fergal seemed to look at nothing, or at something Ceri couldn't see. Then he said, 'It sounds like the Gaelic word for seal.'

'*Oh*,' Ceri said, and then wished she hadn't been so interested, for Fergal's gaze dropped and fastened hawk-like on her. 'What of it?' he asked.

'Nothing. Nothing much.'

He looked at her from under raised eyebrows, and added casually, 'Also, MacMorran means "son of the seal's servant". Probably.'

Ceri swallowed, and said, 'So?'

'As you say,' Fergal drawled, 'nothing much. Probably.'

She changed the subject. 'Do you know a lot of Gaelic?'

Fergal looked suddenly, unexpectedly, embarrassed. 'Not really. I try to learn it sometimes. Some phrases stick.'

'Such as?'

'Oh – *ceol na mara*.'

'What does that mean?'

'Music of the sea. But I only remember that because it's the name of a house round here. And *gait na mara* means laughter of the sea. Laughter of the waves.' He turned. 'Those mountains – that region – the Gaelic name might have been Suinard. Which means, the Sleeping Heights.'

'Nice,' Ceri said.

'Interesting,' Fergal said firmly. He was silent for a little, and then said, 'If you really like seals, I saw a good one for sale yesterday – carved, you understand. It was in the jetty shop over at Salen. Like to come and have a look at it?'

'Please.'

They sat inside the strawberry ice-cream car and stitched their erratic course zig-zag along the loch shore. The bright sun behind the leaves gave the road a green roof, but underneath it the tunnels and pale tree-trunks kept their air of mystery, as if they were the places where the old stories had been acted out.

68

Seven

They came out of the dark woods on a road that curved down to a stone jetty. Fergal swung the car to a halt, and reached across Ceri to open the door. 'Sorry,' he said. 'It's quicker for me to do it than explain how to get the knack.'

They got out of the car. There was seaweed black round the edge of the water – Ceri could smell it like all the seaside holidays she had ever had – and a stack of empty lobster-pots and fish-crates against the wall of a hut. With its creosoted planks it looked nothing like a gift-shop, but Fergal walked straight inside and said, 'Here it is.' He turned towards Ceri and handed her a slip of wood that seemed too light in her hand to be anything: but she looked at it and saw a perfect small seal, carved in pale wood with black inset eyes.

'I love it,' she said. 'But I left my money at the house.'

'You could come back later.'

'I could.' But Ceri was suddenly consumed with the need to buy the seal now, not to leave it behind, in case some less worthy tourist came in and snapped it up. Her fingers closed a little, protectively, round it.

Fergal said, diffidence tingeing his voice, 'I could give you a lend out of my wallet. If you really want it.'

'Oh, *yes*, but – ' The 'but' was too late. Fergal was at the counter.

They came out and blinked in the sunshine, Ceri holding the seal in its box-and-tissue wrapping, Fergal shading his eyes with one hand. He said, 'That looks like Euan. With the yacht Aunt Morag was clacking about.'

The yacht was close inshore, sails quivering as she changed course. All that could be seen of anyone on board was a slice of body and arms between the bottom of the sails and the top of the cabin.

'How do you know it's Euan?' Ceri asked.

'I have no proof he's aboard, you understand,' Fergal said, grinning. 'But I recognise the yacht. Ahoy, *Saltair*!'

The yacht turned as if she had heard him, sails slapping taut, and next moment was alongside the jetty. Euan stepped round the swinging canvas and did something to a rope that seemed to spill the wind out of the sails, while Fergal fended the hull off from the stone. 'Hi, Euan,' he said. 'Stopping?'

'Only for a refuel,' Euan said, knotting a blue rope round a ring-bolt. 'Engine all day – they wouldn't have the sails up, because Madam felt sea-sick with more than two degrees of list.' He went up to negotiate with the shop, and presently the smell of petrol joined the fish and the seaweed.

Euan put the nozzle back up, shaking his hands with the distaste of a cat that has got accidentally into water, and said, 'Come for the ride?'

'Can't, I've got the clockwork marshmallow with me,' Fergal said. 'What about you, Ceri?'

'I have to go back.'

'It's on my way,' Euan said.

'And I owe Fergal some money.'

'As if that couldn't wait,' Fergal said grandly. 'Get along with you.'

'Well – thanks.' She pushed the seal in its box deep into her pocket, took Euan's offered hand, and stepped off the jetty and over the rail of the boat, landing inelegantly on the deck. She paused, and blinked. That reminded me of something.

'What's wrong?' Fergal asked.

She looked at him, surprised. What had he noticed? 'Nothing,' she said. 'I just remembered my PE teacher saying I move like a moulting crane.'

'Your PE teacher needs glasses,' Fergal said. 'Or maybe a tongue transplant.' He laughed, and went to help Euan loose the moorings: then, leaning on one rope, he pulled *Saltair* to the end of the jetty. The yacht swung out into open water, caught the wind as she drifted from behind the shelter of the trees, and began to tug at the sails like a dog on a lead.

It was much quieter than Ceri had expected; the wind was blowing them along, not passing them, so there was no sound of it in her hearing aids. The yacht's movement seemed easy and fluid; Euan had handed her a buoyancy aid, which she had put on, but she didn't feel as if she would need it. She leaned over the side and watched the blue-and-white water foaming by. Euan was moving barefoot round the deck. He passed her once, and his hand touched her hair, but not as if he'd meant to.

Then Ceri saw something whitish that was not water. She took a closer look.

'Euan?'

'What?'

'There's a seal . . . is it all right?'

In a few strides Euan came to her, looked, and was at the ropes again. He hauled on one of them, and *Saltair* rocked uneasily in what felt suddenly like no wind at all. Euan stepped over the deck rail and dropped into the water.

A few moments later he reappeared, holding the ladder with one hand and climbing carefully, so as not to bump what he was carrying against the side. He laid the seal on the deck and knelt down.

'Not dead, 's it?' Ceri said, feeling her voice shake.

'No,' Euan said shortly. 'Caught up in fishing-line.' He began to tug and wrench at the stuff with his bare hands.

'Shall I get scissors?' Ceri asked. 'A knife?'

But Euan was blocking the way to the hatch, and in any case didn't reply. His lips were drawn back in what looked like a snarl, and Ceri thought the breath might be hissing through his teeth. She noticed that, though Euan was wrestling fiercely with the tangled line, the seal was hardly jolted. Ceri touched his shoulder: he jerked under her fingers as if he had forgotten she was there, and turned to look at her. His eyes were blank with anger.

'Sorry,' Ceri whispered, and stepped back. Euan made some indefinable noise in his throat, took a deep, shuddering breath, and began to unpick the knots with something more like patience.

At last he sat back on his heels, coiling the line loosely round his hand. The seal wriggled, and opened its mouth. Euan relaxed, and rubbed the scruff of its neck. 'You'll be all right,' he said. 'God rot all weekend fishermen.'

'Fergal would say, they have a living to make,' Ceri said.

'Oh, I don't mean the real fishers,' Euan said. 'I mean the Saturday afternoon show-offs with their fancy boats, dropping line around as if the sea was theirs.' He sat still, his hands resting limply on his knees. The seal shuffled closer and laid its chin on his foot. Euan looked down, laughed, and said something in Gaelic.

'Is it a baby?' Ceri asked.

'No . . . but he is young, maybe his first year on his own,' Euan said. He got up, walked over the cabin roof, and hooked the cabin door closed with one foot. 'Can't have you in there.' But the seal seemed perfectly content where it was; Euan nudged it with his foot, and spoke in Gaelic again. The seal looked at him as if it understood, and when Euan lifted the steel cable that was the lower line of the deck rail, it shuffled forward, waited for a moment on the edge, and then dived into the sea. Euan leant over the side to watch.

'Heigh-ho,' he said, after a while. 'Back on course.' He reached for a rope: but let it go almost at once, and flexed his hands cautiously. Ceri saw a narrow snake of blood slipping between his fingers, across his knuckles. 'Your hands!' she said, aghast.

'I know,' he answered. 'It was pulling at that fishing-line did it.'

'You must come back and let me put something on them.'

'I'll survive.'

'Oh, Euan, please! Or I shall worry. And you were taking me back anyway.'

He laughed a little. 'All right, then. But I must do something with these sheets or we'll be here all night.'

Sheets? Ceri looked up at the sails. I suppose you could call them sheets. Large flat white things. 'Use the engine,' she said.

'With a wind like this?' Euan reached for the rope again, winced, and sighed. 'Oh well. Looks messy motoring in with the sails not stowed, but it won't hurt.' He jumped down into the steering well. 'Just belay the mainsheet on that cleat there.'

If sails were sails, then what were sheets after all? Ceri sighed and said, 'You're not speaking my language.' But she didn't mind, the way she would have done if it had been Mum or Michael talking over her head. She walked forward, hoping that was the right direction.

'Sorry,' Euan said, looking up from a gleaming handle. 'Sheet equals rope. Mainsheet is the one by your hand now. Cleat is that shiny bit by the top of the ladder – yes, that one. Twist the rope round it. Thanks.' He bent down again, and the engine started with a cough and chug. Ceri let go the slack end of the mainsheet and, holding on to the rail with one hand, walked gingerly astern. She sat down, her feet dangling in the steering well. Euan was looking ahead, ducking now and then to see under the sails. 'Should have stowed them,' Ceri saw him mutter – there was no hearing over the noise of the engine – and then he jumped out of the steering well, put her hand to the tiller – 'Hold it there' – and went forward. Ceri felt the quiver of the engine through the tiller into her hand; the sails slipped down silently as clouds, and Euan bundled them away. She looked back along the white line that the yacht drew on the water.

'It's gone,' she said.

Euan came back, took the tiller and said, 'What has?'

'The seal.'

74

He looked down at her, smiling slightly. 'Would you stay in range of the enemy? – especially if it was dropping exhaust in your water?'

'But you rescued it.'

'And I might have left the fishing line in the water, for all it knows.'

Ceri tried to look at Euan without his noticing. Did he think she hadn't seen the seal resting its chin on his foot? Or heard him talking to it?

'Can't be too long,' Euan said as he climbed on to the MacInneses' jetty with the mooring line, 'or the ebb will leave me stranded.' Ceri led the way to the house; and when she was indoors realised that Euan was still out on the grass. 'Come in, Euan!'

He stepped forward, hesitated on the threshold, and then came in, warily. Ceri was suddenly reminded of a strange cat, coming into a house where there might be a dog. She turned the cold tap on and said, 'Put your hands under that.'

Euan looked briefly amused. 'Know all about it, don't you?' he said, putting his hands under the running water and wincing.

'It's what Mum always says if I cut myself.' Ceri opened and shut cupboards, moving round the room as if it was a speed test. 'She's hidden the first aid box.'

Euan looked at his hands. 'I'll be all right.'

Ceri stopped beside him and pointed. 'Blood. Stupid man. You'll get tetanus.'

'I never get anything.'

Ceri sniffed. 'If you say so.'

Upstairs the inland door banged open, and a moment later

Mum came briskly down the stairs, almost jumping, the way Sam did when he was feeling cheerful. 'Hi Ceri. What's up?'

'I can't find the first aid box for Euan.'

'In my room, half a moment.' And Mum whisked out again, humming. Ceri stared in amazement. 'What's bitten *her*?'

'The midges round here bath in laughing gas every morning,' Euan said seriously. He took his hands out of the water and sat down at the table.

'That's the first joke I've ever heard you make.'

'And I didn't make it,' Euan said. 'It's one of Fergal's.'

Ceri looked at the narrow red gouges on his palms, and the white edges of torn skin. She picked up the towel. 'I'll dry them. Tell if I hurt.'

Euan sat still while she dried his hands. Ceri had never been so close to him for so long before; but when she looked up at his face, his eyes were unfocused, as if he was thinking about something else, not noticing her at all.

'What were you doing?' Mum asked.

Euan came back from wherever he was. 'Rescuing a seal,' he said with half a smile. 'Nothing sticky, please. It'll come off in the water.'

Mum picked up a bandage. 'I haven't got my lenses in,' she said, peering at the label. 'But this looks all right. Ceri, get the scissors, love.' She wound Euan's hands in bandage, and cut and pinned the ends 'I'm not sure you shouldn't have stitches in that,' she said dubiously.

'They'll need to catch me first,' Euan said. 'Thanks, Mrs Hughes. And Ceri.'

'Stay for tea?' Ceri asked.

He shook his head. 'I must take Ed Collins his yacht back.

Tell Ruth I've gone to Kinloch if you see her.'

'But how will you get home?' Ceri asked, following him through the seaward door. Did she only imagine a sigh of relief as Euan stepped outside?

'Home?' Euan said, as if he didn't know what the word meant. And then, 'Oh, in the dinghy.' He looked at her as they scrunched along the shingle to the head of the jetty. 'Don't worry about me, Ceri.'

'Why not?' she said, but he didn't answer, only untied the mooring line, stepped into *Saltair*, and started the engine. Ceri watched until he was out of sight, then turned and went indoors again. Mum was in the lounge, on the sofa with her feet up and a mug of tea in one hand. Ceri took her wooden seal out of her pocket, unwrapped it, and put it on the glass coffee-table, where it sat on its reflection like a seal on black ice. 'You were very cheerful,' she said.

'John MacInnes has been paying me extravagant compliments.' Mum's eyes wrinkled in a smile.

'But you're married.'

'So is he. And neither of us means anything by it.' Mum raised her eyebrows. 'Don't look so shocked, Ceri! Grown-ups do it all the time. You don't suppose Euan thinks you mean anything by nursing him, do you?'

It was said with a smile, but it hit Ceri like a kick in the stomach. She stared at her mother, opened her mouth to say something; but words had deserted her. She could feel the sounds breaking between her lips before she spoke them, and anyway there were too many words queuing up in her throat. *What if I did mean something?* and besides, Euan's not *like* you. *Or Ruth. What's it to do with you, anyway?* Mum looked at her, suddenly anxious. 'Ceri? Nothing wrong, is there?'

'No,' Ceri said. 'Don' *worry,* Mum.' Holding the words to-gether was too much, almost. 'Going out for a walk. 'Kay?' Her smile must have looked convincing, because Mum smiled back and said, 'Of course.'

On her way through the kitchen Ceri saw the corner of an airmail letter caught in the lid of the waste-paper bin. Auto-matically she tweaked at it, expecting it to be a fragment of the one Mum had torn up.

It was a complete letter. Without a second thought she tucked it into her sleeve, and took it out with her.

Eight

Alone on the springy, sheep-bitten grass, Ceri switched her hearing aids off and tried to imagine herself into her undersea country. She could relax there; what people said and thought and wanted didn't matter. She listened hard for the whale music, the secret songs that the wind sometimes brought to her: but today there was nothing. The sky was clouding over again, and the distant lochs were no longer blue but grey, like silver.

She came over the crest of the slope and found herself above the shore. There had been a landslip here, and a green slice of turf had come to rest near the beach, leaving a ragged stair for her to climb down. Beside the still-raw side of the hill the gorse bushes were in flower, filling her nose with their coconut scent. It was a quiet, sheltered place, with a view of islands. Ceri sat down and wrapped her arms about her knees. Somewhere on the edge of her hearing a bird whispered. She shut her eyes, and felt the earth swing beneath her.

A faint scratching against her arm, almost like a roughness in the material, reminded her of the letter. She pulled it out and stared at it. No sender's address. A pale stamp with an unfamiliar face on it. From the USA, and her mother hadn't even bothered to open it.

Ceri bit her lip. Shall I shan't I? . . . and picked at one gummed corner with a finger-nail. The letter peeled open as easily as if it had never been sealed. She looked at the foot of the page.

Love, and you better believe it, Paul.

So it was from her father. She had half expected that, but even so Ceri felt a sudden shock. It left her gasping yet exhilarated, like diving into cold water. *Here we are at last. Me and my father.* She began at the beginning.

Dear Jen, Never tell your office your vacation address. Here is one happy client, ha ha. Holding out on me, are you? So, you shouldn't bother. You know I don't give up easy. I'm flying over to see Ruth for myself. Of course you want to get together for old times' sake. I have a suite reserved at some place called The Shieling, which they say is the best hotel around. Here's the number, call me. I'll be there by the time you get this. And how is our one cute babe of a daughter?

There was the telephone number, and the last sentence, and that was all. Ceri stared at the number, repeating and repeating its rhythm inside her head until it had worn itself into her memory. Then she damped the gum and closed the letter again, pinching the folds shut, hoping they would stay that way. Just in case, just in case Mum decided to find the letter again and read it after all.

For a long time she just sat there, until the red light through her closed eyelids told her the sun was setting. Time to go. She climbed up to the top of the slope and looked inland again. In the distance the mountains loomed like stone ghosts. They were not sharp and white like the Alps in pictures; instead they were old and dark and rounded. They must have been there before the ice age. Imagine them under ice, under water. What did Fergal call them? The Sleeping Heights. Ceri shivered in the darkening twilight. If she stood there any longer she would turn to stone herself.

She galloped down, feeling the sound of her footsteps thudding up through her legs and jolting her teeth. Whether what she felt was guilt or anger she couldn't tell – the two seemed to be fighting it out inside her. Her mother should have faced up to the letter. She might at least have showed it to her daughter.   Who else had a better right to know where Paul Schaefer was? How dare Mum put her in a position where she had to sneak round reading other people's letters? The guilt came thumping up her throat again.

It was Mum's letter. It was private.

Yes, but she'd thrown it away.

But it was still sealed.

She'll never know, not if you're careful.

You mean, thou shalt not get found out.

Exactly.

Split-hairer, Ceri thought to herself as she ran. Horrible teenager who opens other people's letters. I hate you. She ran harder, stamping the guilt underfoot. He's my father and I have a right to meet him. Then the thought came bursting into her head again: why does it have to be me that asks him? Why has he never asked me?

And supposing I don't like the answer to that one?

On the last slope above the house she stopped to get her breath back. It took ages. She walked slowly down and leaned on the MacInneses' yard fence, watching a kitten playing like thistledown under the window. One of the collies bounded out, barking with all its strength. Through her switched-off aids it sounded like a dog on an old record, distant and crackly.

She turned aside and crossed the path. The windows of the house were blank behind the reflection of mountain, water and cloud. Mum might be indoors watching for her; or she might not. Ceri stood watching the silken heave of the tide under the water's surface, and then turned back and walked in through the seaward door. Nobody in the kitchen, but a mouth-watering smell. The shortest of pauses as she slipped the letter back into the waste bin. For once she looked at the phone with a sort of hope. Now if only Mum and Sam were out . . .

But she came round the door to see them on the sofa. Sam was excavating the remote control from down the side of a cushion; Mum stood up, smiling, mouth open. Ceri hastily switched her hearing aids on, and the blob of sound that was Mum's voice crystallized into, ' – having dinner soon.'

'Very soon?' Ceri said.

'Well – maybe not very.' The television screen flicked into life. Ceri said, 'Bang on the ceiling when you want me, then,' and went upstairs. She shut the door behind her, crossed the room in the dimness, and retrieved the seal skin from where she had left it. She kicked her sandals off and sat down cross-legged, facing out of the window towards the loch. After a moment she took her hearing aids out.

The skin grew warm under her hands as she stroked it, moving almost as if it still held something alive. Outside there was a strange grey light, the waning moon behind clouds, late on a summer's evening in the far north. The wind was blowing now, and the clouds humped and moved across the sky like ghostly whales.

A staccato pattern of quivers in the floor: Mum thumping the ceiling below her. Ceri sighed, stood up, trod barefoot on her hearing aids, and put them in her ears out of harm's way.

In the middle of dinner Mum said, 'John MacInnes tells me there are otters in the bay beyond the Forestry Commission walk. I thought I'd take Sam there tonight – want to come?'

'Other time,' Ceri said. 'If you go again.'

'Oh, we will if we don't see them. Or even if we do. So will you wash up? You owe some drying up from after lunch.'

'I'll do it.' Anything, only go out, go on, quickly, leave me in the house.

When the door banged shut Ceri raced through the washing and drying up with more speed than thoroughness; the things would dry themselves by morning anyway. Then she switched all the lights off, except for the one by the telephone. Mum and Sam might come back early; whichever door they came through, they would switch a light on, and give her warning.

Her hands shook so much that she dropped the amplifier twice before she clipped it on. Could she remember the number? If not, the letter could still be rescued. Probably. Her fingers hovered over the buttons. Do I really want to do this, yes no yes . . .

'The Shieling, Kirsty speaking, may I help you?'

'I want to speak to my – ' Ceri's mouth was stopped by the unfamiliar word. 'Mr Schaefer, please. Paul Schaefer.'

'Certainly, may I ask who's calling?'

'His daughter.'

'Thank you, Miss Schaefer. Putting you through.'

Miss Schaefer, Ceri thought. That doesn't sound like me.

There was a distant click. A man's voice, of course. 'Ruth? That you?'

Ceri blinked. Why didn't I expect that? 'No, it's Ceri,' she said. 'Hallo.'

'Well, *hey*. This is good news.' He sounded delighted. 'This surely is great. How you doing, kid?'

'Oh – oh, I'm fine.' How dry her mouth was. As if she was frightened. Ceri licked her lips.

'You are? Great.' There was a momentary silence, and then Paul Schaefer said, 'Where are you? How about we meet up?'

'I'd like to. I'm here with Mum.'

'Sure. I'll drive round.'

'No!' Ceri said hastily. 'Not here – I mean, Mum doesn't know I'm doing this.'

A chuckle rattled down the receiver. 'So, fine. You fix it how you like.'

'Tomorrow? Afternoon?' Ceri thought hurriedly about suitable places for a rendezvous. He'd be driving. Not too near Ruth's. As far as possible from anywhere Mum might see. 'You know north-east of Kinloch? The road goes right along by the water.'

'I guess I can find it,' her father said resignedly.

'There's lots of space to put the car off the road. I'll walk there.'

'And how do I know it's you?'

Ceri smiled. 'Ruth says I look like you.'

'That's my girl.' He chuckled again.

They arranged a time, said goodbye. Ceri put the receiver down, laid the amplifier beside it and went to sit down on the sofa. She laid her hand on the little wooden seal and stared at the blank screen of the television. Slowly her mouth grew less dry. Well, you've done it now . . . and still her heart thumped and thumped, as if she had been arranging a bank robbery instead of a mere meeting.

The next morning was bright and sunny. Mum and Sam, who had come back late and slightly dispirited from an otterless excursion, wanted to do nothing but lie on the beach beyond the lawn. Ceri was free to do what she liked.

The Kinloch road wasn't so far away, but there was a steepish climb up and down to the place she had in mind. The shore was deserted except for some black and white birds with red legs; they flew off as Ceri approached, red beaks opening and shutting, but she heard nothing. She sat down on a boulder, rounded by sea and weather, that made a comfortable place to wait. A tractor rumbled past: a lorry stacked high with sawn tree-trunks: two dilapidated vans. Ceri tried to avoid catching the drivers' eyes. I must look so obvious, sitting here not doing anything. Waiting, waiting, and what for? A man I've never met. My father. What am I going to say to him? She shifted uneasily on the rock. Supposing I don't like him?

Another forestry lorry passed, and the tractor came back from the other direction. And at last a long black car, streamlined like an undersea creature.

Ceri's heart began pounding again. The car rolled to a halt. The door opened. Almost there. I do so want to know. I *need* to know. But – why am I doing this? She looked up into her father's face.

It was like looking in a strange mirror, or seeing her own

reflection in the water of a deep well. Her father watched her, maybe waiting for her to speak. But words wouldn't come easily, and somehow, she didn't want to be the one to make the first move. At last he said, 'Hiya, kid.'

Ceri lifted her chin. 'I'm sixteen in November.'

He made a wry face. 'So I said the wrong thing.' He rubbed his thumb on his wrist as if the joint was stiff: but went on doing it, in a way that made Ceri think it was only a mannerism. He looked out of place, on a Scottish beach in an expensive suit and sleek black shoes. She tried to look at him without staring.

'I was glad you called,' he said.

'Why?' It was all she could think of to say.

'You need to ask? I want to meet my other daughter.'

'Here I am.' I won't make it easy for him, Ceri thought. After all, why should I? He's had all the time in my life to meet me, if he really wanted to. I won't just give in and be sweet. What does he expect?

Her father grinned uneasily. 'Stonewall Schaefer,' he said. 'Or has your mom been telling you too much about me?'

'What Mum told me about you,' Ceri said, 'would go on a postage stamp. And leave room for the postmark.'

He threw his head back and laughed, but when he looked at her again his eyes, behind the laughter-lines, were restless and wary. 'Jen is the Human Clam, sure,' he said. 'But what about you?'

Ceri shrugged. 'What do you want to know?'

'Oh . . . everything, I guess. How you like high school, what you plan to major in, who your friends are. And so on.'

'I go to an ordinary school,' Ceri said. 'It's no worse than any other. I have no plans, and my friends are ordinary people.'

'But do you like your life?' he asked, and it was such an odd question that Ceri looked at his eyes instead of his lips. He was still watching her intently, almost speculatively. Suddenly she wanted to surprise him; she said, in the best American accent she could manage, 'I guess I've got no option.'

Paul Schaefer said, 'That sounds more like a daughter of mine.' He looked dubiously at the pebbles, hitched up his trousers at the knees, and sat on his heels. 'Suppose we talk.'

So what have we been doing for the last five minutes? Ceri thought: and then he looked up at her, grinned, and said, 'Talk some more.'

'Okay,' she said. 'Dad.'

He looked pleased. 'You don't call the other one Dad?'

'Well – sometimes. Not so much lately.' Ceri sat down on her comfortable stone again.

'Uh-huh,' her father said.

Ceri hesitated – what should she tell him? She didn't get on that badly with Michael, after all. Really she'd only said 'Dad' to try out how it sounded. She said, 'I don't even know what you do.'

'Business,' he said. 'Big business.'

'Fine, but what sort of business?'

'Oh, all sorts. I'm over this way on a contract for a security firm.'

Ceri said, 'I thought you'd come about Ruth,' and knew immediately that she had said the wrong thing. His lips pinched tight, the muscles at the corner of his jaw twitched, and he said, 'Ruth could do real well for herself in the States. She wants to waste her time working for nothing at some weirdo religious outfit, she may as well. She doesn't take any notice of me, and

Jen won't do anything. What chance have I got? I'm only the poor bloody father.'

Ceri's mind went blank. Surely he couldn't mean the Abbey? 'But that's stupid,' she said.

'What did you say?' he snapped.

'The Abbey's famous. It's not weird.'

'All religions are weird,' her father said. 'Nobody but a fool's going to believe in something you can't see.'

Ceri sat silent. Any moment now he's going to ask me if I believe in God. How am I supposed to answer that? I don't even know the answer.

Then her father said, 'Okay, okay, so I lost my cool. Don't do that in business, kid, it loses you deals.'

'Are you always very busy?' she asked.

'Most always.' He looked at her. 'Why ask?'

'I just wondered . . . whether that was why you never came before.' Ceri bit her lip. I didn't mean to sound plaintive like that.

Her father rested his forehead on one hand, pushing his fingers through his hair. She couldn't see his face. 'I guess it was, partly,' he said.

'You must have had rights to see me,' Ceri said. She was a bit vague about the law, but still . . .

Her father looked up. 'I sure did, but you know how it is, fathers and small daughters, I guess I was a bit worried how they might take it . . . and now you're old enough to have your own mind, Jen can hardly accuse me of trying to influence you. Or anything else.' He took a deep breath. 'And I thought it might be better for you. The battle of the ex-es, someone called it. Didn't want you caught up in that.' He picked up a stone from the beach, held it for a moment, and threw it aside.

Ceri glanced at him. Difficult to tell how much he really meant or minded. 'And what now?' she said.

Her father looked at her with a curiously intent, almost puzzled gaze. 'You know something . . . you said you were like me. Oh, I thought, she can pay a compliment. I wasn't expecting – you are *so like* me.'

'Am I? Am I really?' She felt absurdly pleased.

'Come and see.' He reached out and pulled her to her feet. They crossed the road and stood by the car. It had smoked-glass windows; in them, like sepia portraits, Ceri saw the reflection of herself and her father. Something about the light, and the tint of the glass, smoothed out differences in their faces. They did look very alike. Behind them the clouds moved slowly.

Paul Schaefer said, 'I wasn't going to, but I will . . . see here, Ceri, after you called last night, I was thinking. I thought a lot. How about you come to the States some time?'

'Wow . . .'

'Like the idea?' He looked pleased again, but what Ceri felt was a sort of blundering surprise. America belonged on television: she couldn't imagine ever being there, behind the screen. 'For a holiday?' she said cautiously.

Her father looked at her as if he was weighing something up. Then he said, 'To live, if you want. Once you're sixteen, you can leave home if you want. That's the law in England, isn't it?'

'I don't know,' Ceri said vaguely, still trying to absorb the suggestion. 'I think you need your parents' permission.'

He laughed. 'You'd have mine!'

'Yes.' Images and thoughts tumbled silently through Ceri's head, television with the volume off; tall glass buildings, prairies, mountains. A confusion of her own ideas about

America, or were they other people's? 'Where do you live?' she asked, trying to pin something down, anything.

'Pennsylvania. PA. You'd like it. Some parts are real pretty. They even cleaned up Pittsburgh.'

She looked away from him, away from the intensity of his gaze, but still the pictures and words crowded behind her eyes. Half of her was American, she would be at home there; but the other half whispered, only in stories are the streets all made of gold. Buildings, people, landscapes; they demanded to be let in, to be made real. All the kingdoms of the world . . .

'But what would I do over there?' she said.

'College. Business. Anything you want. I promise.'

'I don't know . . .' she said.

'I guess you need time. Well, I'll be here a few days. Call me at my hotel again,' he said. 'Or write me in PA, if I've gone back. We'll work something out.' He reached inside his suit. 'Here. My card.'

Ceri read it slowly, and slid it into the pocket of her jeans. Out of the corner of her eye she could see her father's long, narrow hands – like hers, she realised – moving restlessly again, rubbing and rubbing his right wrist as if it ached.

'I ought to go back,' she said, uncertainly.

'Oh?' her father said. 'Am I boring already?'

'No!' Ceri shook her head, laughing, confused. 'Only I don't know what to say.'

He said, 'Then say nothing, kid. Let me take you some place special.'

Round here? Ceri thought. I already have special places. The view from my window. The loch with the seals. 'Not this time,' she said.

'Why not?'

Ceri hesitated. 'Mum might – be expecting me back soon.'

Paul looked at her. 'Did you tell her you called me yet?' There was a gleam of satisfaction in his eyes, as if he already guessed the answer. Ceri shook her head again, and saw his hands clench together in a sudden movement.

Something in her swinging hair caught her father's eye. He reached out and lifted her hair away from each ear, first left then right. 'What are you wearing those for?' he asked, faintly incredulous; the question that usually came with the assumption that hearing aids are only for the old. She had learned to grit her teeth and ignore all the predictable jokes.

'I've had them for years,' she said.

'Sure, maybe, but why have them at all?'

'Meningitis.'

'*What*? – but that's a killer!'

'Well, it didn't kill me.' Ceri was used to the fact that it hadn't; the dangers of the past were remote and unreal, now. She was surprised to see how pale her father was. 'Jen never told me,' he said quietly: and she realised that his pallor came not from shock but from fury. 'My daughter – you're *my daughter*, and she never told me a thing.' He was quite still for a moment, and then said bitterly, 'She told me once *I* was the sort not to forgive. What about her? I wonder would she have invited me to the funeral?'

'There wasn't one to invite you to,' Ceri reminded him. 'I'm all right.'

'You call this, all right?' her father said, tapping the left aid and setting off her tinnitus. Ceri said aggressively, 'Yes I do. And please don't do that again.'

Her father glared straight into her eyes. Then suddenly he laughed. 'Hell,' he said, 'you're my daughter. And how. Okay, so you're okay. What next?'

Ceri moved back from under his hands. 'I don't know. Not yet. Can I call you again?'

'Any time. Any time,' he said expansively.

'Then I will.' She watched him as he checked his pockets for the car key. 'Dad.'

'Uh-huh?'

'Nothing. I – it's nice to meet you.' She stood up as straight as possible.

'Same here.' He stood looking at her, and suddenly bent to put one arm round her shoulders. He smelt of cleanness and expensive aftershave. 'See you, Ceri.'

'See you.' She watched him get into the car. The engine started with an almost inaudible purr, and the car rolled away. Ceri waved, and out of one window her father waved back, sunlight glinting on the gold strap of his wrist-watch.

She climbed back up the slope and headed for the house, feeling as if the knowledge must be sticking out all over her like neon signs: I have met my father. And then – do I smell of his after-shave? Will Mum notice it? Does he still use what he used when they were married? She stopped short. If they were still married. What would it be like? Who would I have instead of Sam? Would they be in America? Would I have caught meningitis?

I wish I hadn't thought of that.

Nine

At the house everything was quiet. Sam was flat out on the lawn, the peak of his baseball cap over his face, his legs turning slowly pink in defiance of the sun-screen all over them. Ceri preferred the cool indoors: she went in, and sat down on the sofa. There was a book she didn't recognise, poems and pictures. She turned the pages, anything to look idle, to look as if she hadn't just met – my father! for the first time in my life! and I sit and read a book as if I was bored.

And there it was. *The Great Silkie of Sule Skerry*. Four verses on the page; she read the fourth, that she had not heard or re-membered.

> 'Then he has taken a purse of gold
> And he has laid it upon her knee,
> Saying "Give to me my bonny young son
> And take ye up your nourris fee." '

Ceri left the book lying open while she disentangled her thoughts from her father. Why should just thinking – or not thinking – be such an enormous effort?

Silkie. She thought it carefully, as if it were a word in a spell. Silkie. The seal with the human body. Or the man with the seal body. I wonder which way round it is? And what does Euan Roane – or MacMorran or whatever his name is – what does he want? What is it about Ruth and him? Could they be, what do they . . . her thoughts flicked from Ruth and Euan, and passed quickly, with eyes shut as it were, over a picture of her, Ceri, and someone, don't ask who; and then to Mum and – Dad. They must have, once, or I wouldn't be here. And now, well, look at them now. Is Mum right about him not forgiving? What about her, and what am I letting myself in for?

Mum walked briskly by, stopped, and reached for the book. 'There it is. I knew I'd put it down somewhere.'

Ceri reached out, closed her fingers on air, and said automatically, 'I was reading it.' And then wondered what her mother would say if 'I was thinking about you and my father' had come out of her mouth instead. She shut her lips firmly, in case the words got the better of her. Like shouting swear words in church – you don't want to, but you really have to sit on the urge.

'Were you?' Mum said. 'I've got to catch the post, though, or at least catch John MacInnes on his way to Fort William, which comes to the same thing. This is for Hannah's birthday.'

Ceri sniffed. 'Cousins.'

'We choose our friends, God chooses our relations,' Mum said cheerfully.

What about husbands? Ceri wondered. She said aloud, 'He's got bad taste,' and Mum laughed.

'You know you like Hannah really,' she said, 'and talking of friends, you have another invitation from Fergal, or it may be from Ruth, I suppose.'

94

'What this time?'

'Picnic lunch on the beach. Fergal said to meet him here.'

Ceri said something which was meant to be 'Tomorrow?' but came out wrong.

'Try again,' Mum said. 'Have you been practising lately?'

'F – uh, bother practice,' Ceri said, remembering just in time how Mum had reacted when she last swore. 'When? Picnic.'

'Tomorrow.'

Fergal arrived just before midday, not in the clockwork marshmallow but on foot, a bag in each hand. Ceri was waiting for him by the gate. 'Hi.'

'Hi. I would wave if I could, but I can't,' Fergal said, nodding to Ceri's mother. 'You ready? Come on, then.'

He led the way to the hollow in the cliff where Ceri had sat two evenings ago. The scent of the gorse was heavier than ever on the warm air. There was no wind, and small waves fell tentatively across the pebbles. After she had been sitting there for a few minutes, watching Fergal build a fire, Ceri said, 'Will you tell me more about – the stories?'

'Maybe I don't believe them today,' Fergal said blandly.

'Not what you were saying before,' Ceri reminded him.

'I never think the same two days running,' said Fergal, striking a match. 'Excellent training for a course in critical theory.'

'Don't know what you're talking about.'

'Practising for university.' He rummaged in the bags, and brought out a frying-pan and some butter.

'And you haven't answered my question.'

'That too is practice,' Fergal replied, looking innocent. Ceri gave up, for the moment. She watched the fire grow. Fergal began sliding a lump of melting butter round the pan with an elegant movement of his wrist. He put it down, turned aside to one of the bags, and said, 'Move it off the fire if it sizzles.'

'I won't hear it.' Ceri had stood near a frying-pan before; the noise was almost exactly the same as what she lived with in her ears anyway.

'Then watch for it to spit,' Fergal retorted. 'Not too closely, of course.' He dug in the bag. 'I'm about to do horrible things to these fish – mind you, they're dead already – so don't watch if you're squeamish.'

'I do think life is horrible,' said Ceri, watching the melted butter intently.

'Life,' Fergal said, obviously speaking up because he was looking away from her, 'is a matter of survival, as you'd find out if you spent a winter up here instead of in the cosy South. *And* you'd eat these fish guts and all – if you were a seal.'

'But I'm not.'

'No,' he said.

Ceri hovered on the brink of asking, 'Is Euan?' But under the bright daylight and clean wind the question seemed stupid. Whatever she had convinced herself of before. In the end, she said, 'I've read *The Great Silkie* now. All four verses.'

'Four?' Fergal said. 'There are six. Seven if you include the one they usually leave out.'

'Oh damn. And Mum posted the book away.' She looked at the pan. 'It's spitting.'

'Move it off the flame, would you?' Fergal turned round, holding some fillets; they bore no relation at all to fish anatomy, she was pleased to see. He laid them in the hot butter, and there was an instant smell of cooking.

'That song,' Ceri said. 'What's it really about?'

'Oh, there's a deal of words wasted,' Fergal said, 'in books, you know. That the silkie would be stealing the woman away.'

'Would he?'

'Who knows? Maybe.' Fergal turned the fillets over, and said, 'Where's your sister? She'll get nothing but the bones if she's any later.' And then he didn't wait for an answer, but asked, 'What would you do if you saw something impossible?'

'Keep watching,' Ceri said. 'What about you? Why ask?'

Fergal laughed. 'Pass. I was just checking.'

A shadow fell across their hands. 'Checking what?' said Ruth.

'Never you mind,' Fergal said. 'You're just in time for frizzled fillet.'

They picked their way to a hump of grass that had come down with the landslip, and sat on it in a row; but Fergal got up at once and said, 'I forgot the drink. Half a moment.'

Ruth cut her fish up with her fork and said, 'So what did he just ask you?'

'What I'd do if I saw something impossible,' Ceri said, finding a bone and flicking it off her fingers. 'What would *you* do?'

Ruth laughed. 'Rub my eyes and look again.'

'And if it was still there?'

'Then I'd believe it.' Ruth smiled, and fell silent for a moment. She spoke again, and Ceri was not quite sure whether she was continuing the last part of the conversation or starting a new one. 'I remember the first time I saw Euan. I came outside real early, the sun was up but it didn't get above the mountains yet. Anyway so the shore is dark and the sky isn't, and there I am, and Euan walks out of the water.'

'What did you think?' Ceri asked shyly.

'Think? I didn't,' Ruth said simply. 'I was just – gone on him. At once. Like lightning. You wouldn't know.'

Ceri hugged her knees and thought about it. Wouldn't I? That's what you think. She wondered if Ruth knew *The Great Silkie* – she had been at the ceilidh – but no, it had been the first song and Ruth had arrived during the applause. Slowly Ceri asked, 'Ruth . . . you're not pregnant, are you?'

Ruth laughed out loud. 'I am not! I hope I'm not so stupid. And what gives you the idea, anyway?'

'I – I don' know,' Ceri said, covering her confusion by letting her words fall to pieces. 'Something. You look happy so much.'

'Nice compliment. Wrong deduction,' Ruth said, smiling. 'Where's that boy gone with the drink?'

'He's coming back,' Ceri said, licking fish from her fingers. Then she said, 'Where is Euan?'

Ruth said to Fergal, 'Did you remember the corkscrew?'

'Of course I did, woman. The Scots are a practical nation.' Fergal took out the corkscrew with a flourish and set to work; and Ruth said, 'Euan's out on *Saltair* again. He said if we saw him come home we could go call on him.'

'Home?' Ceri said. Euan still hadn't told her where he came from.

Ruth pointed to where, in the distance, a dark shape crouched on a headland. 'That cottage is his.'

'Have you been there?'

Ruth looked faintly puzzled. 'Now you ask, no, I haven't. I always meet him when I'm on my way there.'

Ceri jumped. 'What was that noise?'

'Didn't you recognise it?' Fergal said incredulously. 'Haven't you heard a cork coming out of a bottle before?'

'Mum doesn't drink.'

'*Dia*,' Fergal said. 'What you've been missing. Will I pour you some wine? Or there's orange juice.'

'Orange juice,' Ceri said, after a pause while she swallowed a mouthful of fish.

'Why didn't you learn sign language?' Fergal said. 'Then I wouldn't have had to wait for an answer.'

'Mum said I didn't need to,' Ceri said.

'You should,' Ruth said, laying her plate aside. 'In the States it's a language option in high school – lots of kids learn it.'

'But not here,' Ceri said. 'And I didn't say I didn't want to. Mum said I didn't need to, and that was that. I'd learn it if I could.' She handed her plate over silently for more fish, and went on, 'They thought it would be a good idea if I went to a club for the deaf. So I went. Full of people doing nothing but sign. Ignored me because I couldn't.'

'Surely not,' Ruth said.

'How do you know? And anyway, why should I go be separate? Teenager just like the rest,' Ceri said, feeling language skid on her tongue as it so often did when she started to get angry. 'Too deaf to be hearing and not deaf enough to be deaf.' She gulped down some orange juice.

Ruth touched her lightly on the arm and said, 'Okay, sis.'

Ceri turned towards her and smiled. Ruth was so unlike their father – not remotely similar. How strange to start knowing your sister properly after all these years. How strange to be so different from her. Like my father, different from Ruth . . . isn't she like him at all?

Movement beyond Ruth's shoulder caught Ceri's eye. It was Euan, rowing. He crunched the dinghy into the pebbles with less than his usual care, climbed out, and hauled it up the beach.

Ruth said sharply, 'Euan, you're soaked – your hair's dripping.'

'Yes,' he said, dropping down beside her. The light glinted on the curve of his shoulders.

'You've been swimming.'

'Had to go after the dinghy. Stupid of me. Slipped her moorings while I was out with *Saltair*.'

'But you promised me,' Ruth said, with no particular anger, only a quiet, dull misery in her voice that Ceri couldn't understand.

'Oh Ruth – not now,' Euan said wearily. He lay down with his head in her lap, took her arm and laid it across his shoulders. Ruth was still for a moment; and then steadily, rhythmically, her fingers began moving, stroking the nape of Euan's neck. The glass of wine in her other hand tilted sideways. Euan took it, swallowed the wine, and closed his eyes. Ceri bit her lip and looked away.

Fergal began to collect the dishes, and picked the frying-pan up from the pebbles. Ceri finished her orange juice, and the last of her fish, and picked up the glasses for him. They walked away together; nobody said goodbye.

'Thanks, Fergal,' Ceri said, when they were over the top of the slope. 'That was good.'

'It was all right, wasn't it?' he said. 'Some day I'll learn another recipe. Fish is about all I can cook.' He turned and looked back towards the beach. 'Hope they make sure the fire's out before they go.'

'Didn't look as if they were going anywhere soon.'

'No,' Fergal agreed. They looked at each other. Was there anything to say? Nothing that wasn't obvious. Ceri smiled tentatively, Fergal shrugged, and they walked on. 'I'll wash up at Aunt Morag's,' Fergal said.

'Come and give you a hand,' Ceri offered.

'Three of everything, and one pan? Hardly worth it,' Fergal said. 'But thanks for the offer. So when they reached the farm he went down one path and Ceri down another. Into the quiet house, and an afternoon and evening still as the day's wind; only her thoughts weren't still. In her room Ceri put 'Chansons secrets des baleines' into her cassette player. Played it, and turned it round, play, and around, until she went downstairs and sat listening to the television, not hearing very much, but anything to have human voices in her ears.

The phone rang in the kitchen. Mum turned the television sound off and went to answer it. Ceri could see her, through the open door, making herself comfortable on a chair before picking up the receiver – and then she sat suddenly forward, hunched over the phone, the fingers of her free hand pushed up through her hair and digging into her scalp. Mum's face was hidden, Ceri could not hear a word she said. And yet . . . she sat up straight, and flapped her hand urgently at Sam. 'Who is it?' she mouthed.

Sam pulled his headphones away from one ear and said, 'What?'

Ceri jammed her fingers against her lips for silence. 'Who?' she mouthed again, flicking her hand into a telephone shape.

Sam shrugged, and seemed to be about to sit back in his chair, but then he looked sharply towards Mum; glanced at Ceri, and shook his head.

'*Tell me!*' Ceri said voicelessly, trying to look as urgent as she felt. And slowly, using the smallest possible movements of his hands and fingers, Sam picked a name out of the manual alphabet. P-a-u—

Before he could reach the fourth letter Ceri was out of her chair and beside the telephone. The amplifier was where she had left it last time: she grabbed it, turned the volume of her left hearing aid up, and stood waiting for a chance to speak. If Paul heard she was there, Mum could hardly pretend she wasn't. And if Mum hung up; then all he had to do was call back and keep calling, till he had driven Mum crazy with it.

'I've nothing more to say,' Mum said sharply.

Her chance. 'Can I have a word, then?'

Mum jumped, and nearly dropped the phone. For a moment Ceri thought she was going to lose her temper: instead she stood up, slapped the receiver into Ceri's hand as if she would have liked to hit someone with it, and said, 'Go ahead.'

Ceri slipped the amplifier on. 'Hi, Dad.' There was a gust of wind behind her, and the air quivered. Her father chuckled. 'That was some bang. Has your mom stomped out of the house?'

Ceri looked behind her. 'Yes.'

'As from one American to another,' her father said, 'that's how Jen deals with a situation she can't handle.'

'Sam's still here,' Ceri said, meaning, I'm not going to agree with you in public.

'Sam? I thought his name was Michael.'

'Oh – no. I mean yes, Michael is – ' Ceri stopped, unhappily aware of Sam in the corner of her vision, his headphones on his knees, listening. There was silence at the other end of the line.

Sam stood up, said loudly, 'Michael is my father,' and went out too; leaving the door open.

'Did you hear him?' Ceri asked.

'Sure I did. What's he like?'

'He's a brother.'

'Enough said, huh?' There was an odd rustling on the line, and Ceri had a sudden vivid picture of her father rubbing the mouthpiece of the telephone, his hands restless as she had seen them when he stood on the beach in front of her. She said, 'Can I come and see you? At the hotel?'

'You take the invitation from my mouth. Spend the evening, have dinner. Okay by you?'

'Dinner?' Ceri said uncertainly.

'Candle-light, the works. Only the best for my daughter.' There was a warmth in his voice that she could not mistake, even through the amplifier.

'Okay by me,' she said. 'When?'

'Tomorrow at six. I'll pick you up where we met before.' There was not the hint of a question in his voice.

'You work so fast!'

'Only way to do business, kid. Is it a deal?'

'It's a deal,' she said. 'See you at six tomorrow.'

Ceri put the receiver down, took the amplifier off, and went back into the lounge. A moment later Sam came quietly in from the hall and sat on the sofa beside her.

'Good thing Mum went right out,' he said. 'She'd go spare if she heard you just now.'

'Bet she's not too pleased you told me it was him,' Ceri said.

Sam shrugged uneasily. 'She hasn't been back to ask yet,' he said. 'If this was home I'd have said she was down the off-licence getting ten low-tar and ignoring the alcohol.'

As if he had conjured her up, Mum came in through the upper, inland door, and down the stairs, heels clicking irritably. She said to Ceri, 'How did you know it was Paul?'

'I guessed,' Ceri said. 'Who else would make you act like that?'

Her mother laughed, not very convincingly. 'Fair enough. So what are you going to do?'

'Nothing,' Ceri lied. Sam glanced at her, and she said again, fiercely, '*Nothing*. What should I do?'

'Oh God,' her mother said, 'I don't know. You could try throwing Paul over a cliff. That would solve all our problems.' And she laughed again.

But not mine, Ceri thought. Not mine.

Ten

Mum's laughter trailed dryly into the silence. The three of them looked at each other for a few moments. Then Mum said, 'I meant to go out and look for the otters again. But I don't suppose you're interested in coming.'

'Yes I am,' Ceri said.

'Me too,' Sam said. 'Otters are cool.'

Mum grinned. 'Quite. Okay. Woolly jumpers and rubber soles. And bring your torch, Sam, will you?'

'Can I leave my aids behind?' Ceri said. 'It's dark nearly.'

'Oh – I suppose so,' Mum said. 'Look, you both go and get ready – and don't forget the midge-repellent. I'll put some coffee in the flask.'

When Mum pulled the car in at the side of the road and switched the headlights off, Ceri sat blinking in the dark for a moment, waiting for her eyes to adapt to the night. Sam was already scrambling out of the car, but Mum too sat still for a moment, as if she were thinking of something else. Then she opened the car door. 'Come on, Ceri.'

Ceri and Sam followed her off the road and along a path

springy with moss. Sam flicked the light around, showing a tracery of branches ragged with lichen. Mum, one hand holding her hair down to stop it catching, ducked under a web of leaves and tendrils; Ceri followed her, and walked into the scent of honeysuckle, so strong it seemed she should be able to touch it. There was a pale gleam in front of her, the light shining on Mum's face as she looked back. Her mouth was moving. Ceri looked at Sam. He shone the light on his lips again, mouthed 'Follow Mum' so exaggeratedly that she could hardly make it out, and stood there waiting for her to go on.

Mum was wearing dark clothes, and what Ceri could see best was her fair hair; so she followed that. When they came to a patch of short turf Mum walked forward slowly, and then lay down full length. Ceri lay down beside her, and a moment later felt a quiver in the ground as Sam joined them. She thumped the turf in front of her: it vibrated almost as if it were hollow.

Slowly the shifting darkness resolved itself. Once Sam had switched the light off it became easier to make out detail, shades of grey and the flicker of moving water. The pale smudge out of the corner of her right eye was Sam's hair, that had flopped down over his forehead when he propped his chin on his interlaced fingers. Ceri tried to read Sam's watch sideways, straining to see the faint luminous figures. How long had they been there?

Her mother's head went up: she must have heard something. Ceri watched her hands – yes, she was pointing. Ceri looked, saw nothing. Then Sam tugged her sleeve, and pointed again. A fluid black shape ran down a tumble of rocks that trailed into the water just below them; and another one.

Ceri lost track of the time they watched the otters: but when at last Sam sneezed and scared them off, she realised how very stiff she was. She got awkwardly to her feet, blinking as Sam accidentally shone the light in her face.

They sat in a line on a fallen tree-trunk and drank coffee, sharing the cup from the thermos flask because Mum had forgotten the others. Ceri was waiting for it to come her way again when she saw movement in the distant water.

'Mum – Sam. Look – look!' She jumped up and ran forward.

Mum strolled over. 'What is it?'

'Seals. Two of them. Do look.'

Mum stood beside her for a while, without saying anything, watching. Then she shivered, said, 'I need some more coffee,' and went back to Sam.

Ceri stayed where she was. The seals swam liquid and glinting as quicksilver through the dim water. *I could watch them for hours. What it must be like to swim with them.* Ceri walked as near to the edge as she could, for a closer look; and something made her look down past her feet to the shallow drop below.

Surely she could not be mistaken. There was someone there, crouched down in the shelter of the headland, watching the seals too.

'Euan,' she said softly.

He turned his face up to hers so quickly that she hardly needed to imagine the sudden indrawn breath. She saw his hand move – a finger across his lips – and then he flattened himself against the overhang of turf.

A hand touched her arm. 'Are you coming, or do we stay here all night?' Sam's lips said in the circle of light. 'It's one o'clock.'

Ceri slept all the next morning, and came downstairs in time to have lunch for breakfast. Mum had dark lines under her eyes, but she said brightly over the salad, 'Did you enjoy yourself last night?'

'Lots.'

Mum nodded. 'You always were – wild about wild animals,' she said, with an upward turn of the lips to acknowledge the feeble pun. 'Right from when you were little.'

'Was I?' Ceri said. 'I don't remember.'

'Don't you?'

Ceri shook her head. 'Everything – on the other side, of being ill, I hardly remember.'

Mum looked at her as if this was news. Ceri supposed it might be. They so rarely talked about what she actually thought about not hearing everything. Only what to do so as to hear as much as possible. Even when it wasn't worth hearing.

'Do you remember – anything, at all?' Mum said.

Ceri stared at her. Oh, why wait till now to ask? Slowly she said, 'I remember . . . when we lived in Dorset. Sam and – and Michael were at home with colds, so we went out together, just you and me. You took me to – I don't know where it was. An artificial hill or something.'

'Maiden Castle,' Mum said automatically.

'Was it? Anyway, we walked around on the top of it for ages, and there was this lovely noise in the sky that you said was the larks singing.'

Mum's lips twitched, as if they held a memory of tears. 'I wish I could give you it back, Ceri.'

And what do I say to that? Ceri thought. What do I want?

'What would I do with it?' she said. 'I have this life now. It suits me.' A memory, sharp as the glint of sunlight on a watch-strap, crossed her mind. Her father. He had offered her another life. If: if she wanted it.

Mum said, 'If it suits you – then that's all right.' She paused, and made as if to say something else. There was a troubled look in her eyes; somewhere there were unanswered questions. Ceri turned and walked out of the kitchen. The cold breath on the back of her neck couldn't possibly be, but still she felt as if it was, Mum sighing. Ceri shrugged it off. She was going to see Euan.

She found him in the hollow of the shore where she had read Paul's letter, and picnicked with Fergal and Ruth. He was fast asleep, curled over the grassy hump with the abandon of a cat in sunlight. Ceri got down cautiously, trying not to wake him, but almost at once he sat up, not blinking or yawning or stretching as anyone else would who had been asleep in the open air on a warm day. 'Hallo.'

She couldn't think of anything to say. At last she pointed to the distant headland. 'Ruth told me that's your home.'

'You might say that, Euan said.

Ceri looked at him. 'You're just trying to be mysterious.'

At that he grinned. 'Do I have to try?' It sounded like one of Fergal's jokes. She threw a pebble at him: he fielded it neatly, and balanced it on top of another. 'So where do you belong?' Ceri asked.

'Nowhere much,' Euan said, perhaps a little sadly. He clasped his hands around his knees. 'Why do you ask?'

'I want to know you.' The words slipped out of Ceri's mouth before she'd sorted them out.

He turned his head and gave her a long look. Ceri shifted in her place: the balanced pebble slipped and fell with an inaudible clatter to join the others on the beach. 'Where do your parents live?' she asked nervously.

'My mother lives on Orkney,' Euan said. 'My father came from – an island in the north. You wouldn't know it.'

'Came?' Ceri said tentatively.

Euan nodded. 'He's dead. A long time ago. I was very young . . . I haven't seen my mother for years. She married again.'

'So did mine,' Ceri said. 'But my father's not dead.'

'No,' Euan said, 'I know that. He's Ruth's father too.'

'Sometimes I think it's like chemistry,' Ceri said, 'or a bit like. You know – chemical bonds. All that. And people treat it like an experiment. Sometimes it works and sometimes it doesn't.'

'Yes, well.' Euan's mouth twisted a little grimly. 'Sometimes you get an explosion and sometimes you don't. It was my mother's second husband shot her first one.'

'*Euan!*' Ceri sat bolt upright, wishing she had kept her questions to herself.

'He said it was an accident.' Euan brushed his hair back from his forehead with a hasty movement of one hand. 'But he – oh, no matter. Talk about something else.'

'I don't think I can.'

'More fool me.' Euan stood up and walked ankle-deep into the sea. Although he had his back to her she could still hear him perfectly. 'Ceri. There are no exact parallels. Things don't happen twice. It may look as if they do . . . but what I'm trying to say is – don't map your life by mine.'

110

'What you mean is,' Ceri said, 'I mustn't go around, because of what you just told me, thinking Michael is going to shoot – my father.' How strange those two words still were; my father. She stood up and kicked her sandals off.

Euan turned towards her, the light glinting in his eyes. 'I suppose I might have meant that,' he said. 'But – ' Whatever he had been going to say, he stopped.

'But, what?'

He frowned, and said slowly, 'I keep thinking I need to warn you. I don't know why. I – '

'About my father?' Ceri bit her lip. 'You've never even met him.'

Euan smiled slightly. 'No? . . . he was with the party I took out on *Saltair* before you came aboard. Five minutes and I hated his guts.'

'Oh!' Ceri felt winded, breathless. Tentatively, trying to shape a laugh, she said, 'You're not serious.'

'Don't tell Ruth,' was all Euan answered.

'I won't.' They were standing close together now: Ceri looked up at him. 'I came looking for you to ask a few things. And – if you would take me swimming.'

'With the seals?'

'How come you know what I'm thinking?'

He smiled. 'This one was obvious . . . but I can't. I'm sorry.' As Ceri turned to him with the question on her lips, he stopped her with his hand outstretched. 'I promised Ruth. After that time. I really did promise.'

'So what were you doing last night?'

'Just looking,' Euan said abruptly, and turned his face away. He stood quite still, the wind whipping his hair about his head.

111

Ceri said, 'You don't seem like the sort of person who breaks promises.'

'No.' He turned towards her again. 'Sorry. Nothing to be done about it.'

'Worse luck for me. Oh well.' She looked at him harder, at the point where the dark hair lifted clear of his forehead. 'Euan . . .'

'Yes?'

'Is that a scar you have on your head?'

His hand went up in the same hasty, almost unconscious gesture she had seen a moment ago. 'Yes,' he said.

Ceri was silent for a while. *Even I can work out that he doesn't want to talk about that. But there are still things I want to know. If only I can ask.* She took a deep breath. 'Who are you?'

He turned slowly and looked down at her. 'Ask nae questions, an' ye'll be tellt nae lees,' he said in stage Scots.

'*Don't,*' Ceri said miserably, meaning, *don't treat me like a stranger, don't laugh at me.*

Euan said nothing.

She had to know. 'Are you—?'

He laid his hand lightly across her mouth. 'Don't say it,' he said. 'Whatever you think you know.' He stepped out of the water.

'But I don't know,' Ceri said. 'Not for certain.' The waves tickled her ankles. Euan, on the beach, looked down at her and said, 'You might be safer that way.'

'What from?' Ceri said, smiling; but Euan turned his back and walked away. Slowly she went to pick up her sandals.

When she got back, Mum was in the kitchen, almost as if she

had been waiting for Ceri to arrive. 'Ceri, love,' she said. 'I asked Morag MacInnes to get this for you when she went for her shopping.' She held out a copy of the book of Scottish songs.

'Oh, Mum – thanks!' Ceri took it, and was visited by yet another twitch of guilt. *She is trying to be nice. How can I think of going out with – Paul?* Ceri remembered with a jolt that she was supposed to be meeting her father at six o'clock. 'What do I owe you?' she asked.

'Nothing. Present.' Mum smiled awkwardly and moved across to the kettle. 'Coffee?'

'*I'll* make it,' Ceri offered. 'You go and sit down.'

'You with your famous hex on all household machinery?' Mum said with a quick smile. It was an old family joke; but quietly the guilt slid away. Ceri moved over to the wall, switched the kettle on, and left Mum to make the coffee.

She took her own mug up to her room when it was made, and sat where the sunlight slanted through the window, wriggling her bare toes against the seal skin. Now where – there it was. She turned the page over slowly, a cold hard noise like a piece of ice sliding. *Too much volume.* She put a hand up to each ear and quietened the world's noise.

There were two more verses.

> 'And it shall come to pass on a summer's day
> When the sun shines bright on every stone,
> I'll come and take my bonny young son
> And teach him how to swim the foam.
>
> And ye shall marry a gunner good,
> And a right fine gunner I'm sure he'll be,

And the very first shot that ever he shoots
He'll kill both my young son and me.'

Fathers and sons . . . Euan had been talking about his father.
And his mother's second husband. With a gun. A gunner.

Ceri swallowed suddenly, and unclenched her grip on the
edge of the book. The gunner had shot – Euan's father. She
heard Euan's voice in her head, louder than the noise in her
ears. 'He said it was an accident. But he – '

But what? The scar on Euan's forehead. Both my young son
and me. Had Euan been *there* when his father was shot? What
had happened to him? Who – what – was Euan's father? 'My
father came from – an island in the north. You wouldn't know
it.' Sule Skerry, Fergal had said. Chunk of rock away out north
from Cape Wrath. 'Things don't happen twice. It may look as if
they do.' Not twice, but – almost?

Where do you belong? she had asked Euan. Nowhere much;
neither on sea or on land. Betwixt and between. Somewhere on
the border-line, between the tides. Not the silkie, but the
silkie's son.

And here I am. Neither hearing nor deaf, neither English nor
American. Between. Ceri curled up over the book as if it was a
pain she held to herself. How do I find where I belong?

Somewhere in the house a door thudded shut, pulling her back
into this world where she had to live. In a sudden panic Ceri
pulled her feet under her, ready to stand up, and looked at her
watch. Five o'clock. Shower, wash her hair, dress. Could she do
it in time? What was she going to wear?

Of course she hadn't come on holiday expecting to go out to

dinner. Showered, and with her hair sticking out round her head like a damp chrysanthemum, Ceri rummaged through her wardrobe. Black trousers – smart enough, just. Strappy sandals. God, no nail varnish. Black top. What else?

I wonder what Mum's brought with her . . . there's that turquoise silk jacket she never goes anywhere without.

It was there in Mum's wardrobe; had been made for someone taller than Mum, so she always wore it with the cuffs turned back. Hastily Ceri turned them down again and shrugged the jacket on. Fits, hooray. She battered her hair into submission with the brush, borrowed – used – a squirt of Mum's perfume, pushed her feet into something more comfortable for walking, and was half out of the inland door before she remembered: if I just disappear they'll have forty fits.

Scribble a note. 'Taken out for dinner, back late, don't worry.' If Mum asks who – cross that bridge when I come to it.

Out of the door again. Over the heather and the wiry grass, a glance behind to see whether anyone was rushing out of the house to fetch her back. Up the slope, into the wind roaring in the microphones of her hearing aids. Ceri galloped down towards the Kinloch road, strappy sandals knocking against each other in her hand; and sunlight gleamed on black paint as her father negotiated the last bend. Just in time.

Eleven

Ceri kicked off her comfortable shoes and pulled the strappy
sandals on, bashing her knees against the glove compartment as
she did so.

'Like me,' Paul said, taking his eyes off the road briefly to
watch her contortions round the seat-belt. 'Long legs.'

'Mm.' Ceri got into a more comfortable position with a sigh
of relief, and the car wallowed round the next bend as her father
hauled on the steering wheel. Fergal had driven with the
panache of local knowledge: Paul drove showily, too fast for the
roads in a car too big for them, making no allowances. Once or
twice Ceri closed her eyes: but it was a shame to waste the view.
They were going along the other shore of the loch from her
drive with Fergal, with the Sleeping Heights beyond the water.
One or two caps of snow floated like clouds on the highest
summits, even this late in the summer. She was glad of the view;
it gave her an excuse not to look at her father. But she glanced
at him once or twice all the same. His face was unreadable.
Maybe he was concentrating on the road, but suddenly it
seemed to her that he wore a mask of strangeness, and stored

behind it all the words he had never said during her childhood.

Paul stopped the car with the hand-brake, in front of a hotel that looked like an escape from a film set. Ceri was quite prepared, as she climbed the steps with her best elegant walk, to find the hall a nightmare of brown panelling and stags' heads. What she didn't expect was what she found: cream-coloured textured walls, subdued lighting, thick springy carpet. There was a glass case in the lobby, full of jewellery sparkling in the display light. Ceri stood at her father's elbow as he collected his room-key. He had the air of casual importance that she always admired in other people but never dared to summon up. She could almost hear her mother now – 'Don't show off, Ceri.'

So how did Paul do it? And the girl at reception, the assistant manager beside the lift, the maid in the corridor – how they all had the same expression. A deferential smile, and a gleam of satisfaction afterwards, like a reflection of her father's manner. Someone important has been polite to me, they seemed to be thinking. Ceri looked briefly up at Paul as they walked along the top floor corridor. And this is my father. Buoyed up by the thought, she smiled at the next member of staff they passed, and was startled to get exactly the same smile and gleam in return.

'Like it?' Paul asked, opening the door.

'Wow,' Ceri said. 'Some view.'

'Not bad,' Paul said, glancing out of the window. 'I meant the suite.'

'We've never stayed anywhere like this,' Ceri said.

'No point to money if you don't spend it.' Paul was bending down to a small cupboard by the television. 'Drink?'

'Uh – orange juice, please.'

'Juice? How's Jen been raising you up?' He twisted the top

off a miniature bottle and emptied it into a glass.

'She doesn't drink.'

Her father stared at her for a moment, said, 'She's changed then. Sure you won't? There's no juice here.'

Ceri moved closer. 'Is that Coke? I'll have some of that.'

Her father turned away to pick up the bottle; and when he turned back, said, 'I asked you a question.'

'I didn't hear you. Sorry.'

A small silence. Paul said, 'There must be something we can do about it.'

'Well, yes.'

'Great! Tell me what.'

'Look my way when you ask a question.'

He laughed, a brusque, irritated laugh. 'Not what I meant. Some other way of fixing it. Like I said, what's money for?'

Ceri said, 'None of me is an it. I'm all me.'

'Okay, sure,' Paul said, with a smile that Ceri suspected meant nothing more than, question shelved till next time. 'What I said was,' he went on, 'where did you get your outfit? I like it.'

'Mostly out of my wardrobe,' Ceri said, glancing down at her front. 'But the silk jacket came out of Mum's.'

'Thought it looked like her style,' Paul said. 'It's better on you, I guess. That blue's too strong for her.'

'You think so? Thanks.' She smiled at him, and took a mouthful of Coke.

Paul settled down in an armchair, stretched his legs and crossed them at the ankle. Ceri pulled the chair out from the writing-table, where a folder of hotel stationery and brochures lay open. As she sipped her drink she looked round the room.

Talk about visible wealth . . . one of the leaflets had slipped out on to the table. She picked it up. Glorious Twelfth, it said.

'What's that mean?' she asked, waving it at her father.

He laughed. 'And you a Brit! Twelfth of August. When the shooting season starts. Firm I'm dealing with has booked us a shoot on a grouse moor.'

'Ugh.'

Paul looked at her, eyebrows raised. 'Heaven's sake, kid. It's only birds. And big business, at that. Don't knock it.'

'Would I dare?' she said, and her father laughed again. 'You wait till I get you to the States. I'll bet you're a good shot.'

Ugh, Ceri thought again. Ugh. Why do they always have to be killing something? She pushed the leaflet out of sight. And then with a sudden thump of her heart, so strong that she couldn't believe Paul didn't see it, Ceri remembered about Euan. I have just found out the most amazing thing in my life and I forget about it for – she looked at her watch – two whole hours nearly.

'Guess you're right,' Paul said, draining his glass and putting it on the floor. 'Time we went down.'

The restaurant was dim, candle-lit, the small flames flickering on every table. Waiters and waitresses, in white shirts with waistcoats and skirts or trousers in some dark material, looked like disembodied pairs of arms drifting about their business. The conditions were less than good for lip-reading. Her father strode easily towards one of the tables marked Reserved; and Ceri crossed her fingers and hoped.

They had not been sitting for long when a pair of white shirt-sleeves floated towards them. The face and fair hair above looked familiar, but before she could see properly her father said, 'Hey, I just had an idea. Stay there.' He pushed his chair back and went out.

'Are you ready to order?' said a voice from above the white shirt-sleeves. It was Fergal.

'What are you doing here?'

'Working, of course. Did you think I led a life of luxury all summer? I shall need something to support my overdraft through university.' Fergal licked the end of his pencil absent-mindedly. 'Will I take your order now?'

'I think I should wait till my father comes back,' Ceri said. She looked at Fergal more closely. 'Is that real tartan?'

'MacInnes, would you believe.'

'So is the boss related to you?'

Fergal grinned widely. 'No. The owner's an incomer. His name is Smith. He wanted to use the Smith tartan –'

'You're joking.'

'Not at all. It was invented by the founder of the Boys' Brigade. Anyway – he didn't have the nerve. So he went into a wool mill and asked for a list of tartans, and they showed him a book with a map of Scotland that had the clans marked on it. He didn't get it quite right, we're a bit north of MacInnes country here; but it comes in useful at Christmas. The place is just covered in the clan plant.'

'Ivy?' Ceri hazarded.

'No, nor mistletoe either, more's the pity,' said Fergal, looking wicked. 'Holly.'

'Because prickly,' Ceri said.

'Never on your life!' Fergal retorted, a look of injured innocence replacing the wickedness. 'Evergreen fidelity it stands for, I'll have you know.' He looked briefly round the restaurant. 'At least I can wear my own name on my badge. See the girl over there?'

'Mm.'

'She's labelled Kirsty. Her name's Lorraine; and Tracey wears Catriona or Janet, depending who's off duty. But they're both as Scottish as me – except to Mr Smith, who wants everything authentic.'

'But don't they mind?' Ceri asked.

'Whiles they think about complaining, but mostly it's too much of a joke. Lorraine's going to put it in a book one day.' Fergal laughed quietly. 'At least they don't have *his* problem.'

'Iain?' Ceri said, catching a glimpse of a passing name badge.

'He had enough of the tourists' attempts at pronouncing Ruareaidh,' Fergal said, spelling it out.

'My father's coming back,' Ceri said. Fergal stepped away from the table, and lifted his notebook again. Paul slid into his seat, glanced up with a smile, and said, 'Five minutes, please. We're not ready.'

'Certainly, sir.' Fergal moved away as if Ceri was a complete stranger: Paul laid a small white package on the table, said, 'What are you having?' and picked up the menu.

'You choose. You know about these things.'

'Okay, kid.' He smiled again. 'Leave it to me.'

It seemed to Ceri, five minutes later when Fergal came back, that her father had deliberately picked all the most expensive items on the menu. And then Fergal said, 'Anything to drink, sir?'

'Mmm . . .' Paul took his right wrist in his left hand, stopped still for a moment, and glanced at Ceri. There was an expression in his eyes she didn't understand. 'I think we'll have champagne,' he said.

'But – ' Ceri began.

He looked at her. 'Aren't we celebrating?'

'I suppose so.' She thought about it for a moment. 'Of course we are.'

'Champagne then,' he said, and turned his face towards Fergal. 'You have any Dom Perignon?'

'One moment, sir.' Fergal picked up the wine list, scanned it briefly, and said, 'We do.'

'Bottle of that, then. I'll open it myself. And mind it's properly chilled.'

'Of course, sir.'

Into the silence while they waited for the first course to arrive, her father pushed the white package towards Ceri and said, 'Something for you, kid. I think you'll like it.'

'Oh, Dad!' Ceri laid her hand tentatively on the paper, and began unfolding it. When the folds sprang apart a little heap of beads lay there, glittering faintly as if they still reflected the blue light from the glass case in the foyer.

'Onyx and lapis lazuli,' her father remarked. 'Shall I fix the clasp for you?' He ignored Fergal, setting the champagne and two glasses down on the table.

'Please,' said Ceri. Her father picked the necklace up and shook it slightly, so that what had seemed like hundreds of small beads dropped into maybe a dozen strands. Ceri leaned across the table while her father reached to do up the clasp. The beads lay around her neck like a cold chain of water.

'I wish I had a mirror,' Ceri said, straining to see if she was reflected in the glass of a picture on the wall. 'Thanks, Dad. Thanks.'

'Never mind the mirror,' her father told her. 'You look just great.'

'Pan-fried haggis,' Fergal said, laying a plate in front of each of them. 'With whisky sauce.' Her father unwired the cork from the champagne bottle, and eased it out. There was a loudish 'phut', but none of the exploding spray that Ceri, who occasionally saw the end of a Grand Prix race when Sam was watching television, had thought was inevitable.

Champagne seemed not to taste of much except fizziness. She wasn't sure if she liked it; but her father obviously approved of it, so she kept sipping. Perhaps she'd better have just one glass.

'Were you ever in Scotland before?' her father asked.

'No,' Ceri said. 'Usually we go to Norfolk.' She looked at him. 'Are you just going to chat?'

'What did you have in mind?' he asked, smiling.

'You've got all my life to catch up on.'

'I know.' He laid his hands firmly flat on the table in front of him. 'I apologise. Look, Ceri, I do. I do. I've not been so good a father, I'm the first to admit it. Won't you let me make up for it now – hey?'

Wow, Ceri thought. Catch Mum admitting her failings. She opened her mouth and said 'Mum – ' just as Paul said 'Jen – ' They burst out laughing, and after that it was easy. She told Paul that her life was too much like any other life to be worth talking about, and in return he told her about America. Into a lull in the talk Ceri asked, 'What would you do if you saw something impossible?'

124

Fergal, bringing the venison-with-rowanberry-sauce, raised an eyebrow; and her father answered, 'If it was impossible it wouldn't be there to be seen. Why ask?'

'Oh – well, why not?'

Her father smiled, and shrugged. 'Guess there's no reason you shouldn't.' He helped himself to green peas. 'Shall I order some Bordeaux to go with this?'

Ceri shook her head. 'Champagne's enough for me.'

He made a wry face. 'You need educating about wine.'

'When I can drink in a pub,' Ceri said.

'So when's that?'

'Eighteen.'

He laughed. 'You could be in the States before then.'

So I could. Ceri watched him as he poured himself some more champagne. He glanced at her, lifting the bottle; she nodded and smiled. Another glass won't do me any harm . . . why did I never spend more time wondering what Dad was like? Why did I never expect him to look like me? Why was I so content to call Michael 'Dad' for so long? She said, 'I wish you'd come before.' She didn't want to sound resentful, but she didn't want him to think she didn't care. 'I do wish.'

'I do myself.' He smiled at her ruefully. 'I didn't know what I was missing. You're an asset and a half, Ceri kid.' He pushed the last green pea round the plate with his fork. 'If I can shape up as a father we'll be fine. Just fine.'

'We sure will,' Ceri said, and they laughed again.

Cloudberry sorbet followed the venison, and coffee followed that, and at last Ceri's father said, 'Even the good times finish. I guess I'd better take you home.'

He left her in the foyer, hovering by the glass cases and

fingering her necklace. Fergal, coming out of the restaurant apparently on business, diverted his course and asked, 'Waiting for a taxi?'

'Dad's gone for his car keys.'

'*What*?' Fergal said.

Ceri said, 'Why shouldn't he? He's my father, remember? – and what's the waiter got to do with it anyway?'

Fergal said angrily, 'I'm not letting him take you home, that's what. How much champagne did you have?'

'Two glasses.' Ceri said. 'Who are you to run my life, Fergal MacInnes?'

'And I'll bet you he had a drink before he came downstairs and finished the bottle – four glasses. And he's going to drive. Don't you know *anything*?'

Ceri stared at him, bewildered by his interference, his unexpected fury; and beginning to be angry herself. She said, 'Mind your own business. I guess it's my own affair.'

'And stop talking American, will you?' Fergal snapped. 'I'm going to finish what I'm doing and then I'll drive you home.' He stalked over to the reception desk, had a word with the manager on duty, and disappeared again. Ceri took a deep breath. Of all the domineering – and he needn't think that because he was older than she was – 'You wait, Fergal MacInnes,' she muttered under her breath. 'You just wait.'

Ceri's father came out of the lift, swinging his car keys in one hand, and went to reception to leave his room key. He was between Ceri and the manager, so she couldn't see what was being said, or even guess at it from their expressions: but finally her father turned abruptly on his heel. 'I am not having my daughter driven home by some half-competent waiter, and I am not prepared to wait.' He was completely furious, but restrained; anger on a cold, taut leash. Ceri looked at him, fascinated. It was impressive to watch. Like lightning. She pushed away the thought of what it might be like if he were ever that angry with her. 'You want me to order a cab, then you should run a service from here.'

Fergal came into the foyer, sober and respectable in a black coat over his waiter's uniform. Her father said nothing, but looked him slowly and coldly over from head to toe. Ceri watched with a flicker of satisfaction. That'll teach him to interfere. 'Can he drive?' Paul asked, without looking at the manager.

'Yes, sir. Of course.'

'There's no "of course" about it.' He looked at Ceri. 'There's a free cab, or there's me. Your choice.'

I'd like it to be him. Ceri glanced at Fergal. But I suppose Fergal is right. She shut her eyes briefly. And if Dad does drive me home then maybe Mum will see him, oh help what am I doing. Deep breath. It's my life. I can see my father if I want to. But the longer I can keep him and Mum apart . . . 'It would be nice if it was you,' she said carefully. 'But I don't want to drag you out at this time of night. And it's not as if you were leaving tomorrow. I'll see you again, won't I?'

'You sure will,' Paul said, grinning. The air seemed to relax. 'Okay, you take your free cab.' He looked at the manager. 'And it had better be a good car.'

The manager's expression was briefly agonized: he disappeared into the office behind the desk, and handed Fergal a set of keys. Fergal's eyebrows twitched, but he went out without comment, and came back in a few minutes.

'Ready, miss?' he said.

'Quite ready,' Ceri replied as coldly as he had asked. She looked at her father: he rested a hand on her shoulder, and came out with her down the hotel steps. There was a black saloon, not unlike Paul's but smaller, standing with its engine running and the doors open. Ceri saw the clockwork marshmallow squeezed into a space in the corner of the forecourt.

Her father said, 'Take care, kid. Be seeing you,' and kissed her goodbye.

They drove sedately out of the hotel grounds. A flash of light from the sign-board at the end of the drive showed Ceri that Fergal's lips were moving. She said, with a kind of vicious satisfaction, 'It's no use talking to me. I can't hear a word you're saying.'

Fergal scrunched the car to a halt, switched the engine off and the inside light on, and said, with his face towards her, 'I don't suppose you realise that I now have to take you home, bring this car back to the hotel, and then get myself home. And I don't know why I bother.' Then he switched the light off, the engine on, and accelerated away.

Twelve

Fergal drove the car into his uncle's farmyard, and left Ceri to get out on her own. She picked her way towards the house in the light from the lounge. The sliding window was still open; she stood nervously, rocking on the aluminium track, feeling the heels of her sandals click against it. What had she forgotten?

'That Fergal's car?' Mum said, looking up from the book on her lap. She was curled up on the sofa.

'No – but it was Fergal.'

'Aha.' Mum smiled. 'Were you out together?'

'Sort of.' Ceri swallowed. 'I borrowed your jacket – couldn't find you to ask.' She took it off. 'I didn't get anything on it. But it might smell of cigarettes.'

The smile widened. 'This is the sort of thing other people's daughters do.'

Ceri smiled back uneasily. If she knew . . . 'I think I'll go to bed.'

'Whatever you like. Cocoa?'

'If you can make it without the gritty bits in the bottom.'

Ceri climbed the stairs feeling as if she had danced the night away, instead of having eaten an expensive meal. Was deceit always so exhausting?

It was a relief to sit down on the bed and reach for the seal skin. She had it on her knees when there was a knock at the door: Sam.

'Cocoa,' he said, and then, 'What's that?'

Ceri half-rolled it up, realised there was no point in trying to hide it now, and said, 'Something Ruth gave me.'

He put the cocoa down. 'And who makes faces about dead rabbits?'

'This is different.'

'Tell me how,' Sam said. When Ceri said nothing he added, abruptly, 'Did you have a good time with – him?'

'You didn't tell Mum?'

'None of my business, is it?' he said. 'She won't half create when she finds out.'

'None of her business, either,' Ceri said uneasily. When Sam had gone she pushed the door firmly shut, and sat down by the window. The moon was in its last quarter, but still gave enough light for her to see someone on the foreshore. Fergal? No, he had driven away. Ceri clenched her fingers in the softness that lay at her side. Outside, at the water's edge, Euan was walking steadily, quartering the beach like a hound on the scent: searching, searching.

Mum was making her first cup of coffee of the day; the smell of it coiled up the stairwell, and Ceri came out of her room to investigate. The inland door was open, and Sam was leaning against it.

130

'Wow,' he said. 'Fergal's tired of pink – he's stolen a car from the embassy. Look at it.'

'Oh my God,' Ceri said, feeling as if her blood had drained out of the edges of her body and clotted round her heart.

'What's up?'

'That's Paul's car. Dad's. My father's.' Ceri tried to whisper. She watched as he swung open the door, stood up, and walked towards her. At her side Sam drew back into the house. Ceri crossed her fingers. If only he would say what he had to, and go. Maybe Mum would never realise.

'Hi! You left these in my car,' Paul said, holding out her comfortable shoes. 'Hallo there, Jen. How you doing?'

Ceri did not look to see what the answer was. I wish you hadn't come here, I wish . . . she couldn't believe he didn't know what he was doing. So he must have done it on purpose. But why? 'Thanks,' she said, taking the shoes. With her eyes she tried to say, not here, not now.

Maybe Paul read the message. He put his hand on her shoulder – what would Mum think of that? – and said, 'Call me when you want me, hey? I can't stop now, I'm due in Stirling.'

'Okay,' Ceri said. She could not stop him kissing her good-bye. And when the car disappeared she had to stifle the impulse to walk away from the house and keep walking, anywhere, out of trouble. Instead she turned round. Sam and Mum were standing side by side.

'Did you have to tell me lies?' Mum said.

'I only told you one. And you mostly thought that one up yourself,' Ceri said defensively. She dropped the shoes by the door and went downstairs, headed for the coffee jug.

'Yes, last night,' Mum retorted, following her down. 'But

what about before? What are you going to do? I asked. Nothing, you said. And you go out with him. I don't call that nothing.'

'*He* took me out for dinner, on my own,' Ceri said. 'I don't remember that you ever did.' She filled a mug with coffee, but put it down again and went back into the lounge. Mum came and stood directly in front of her. 'Stick to the point, Ceri!'

'That is the point. Or some of it.' Ceri looked at her mother. Listen to what I'm saying, she willed her. Listen to what I'm really saying. 'Look at us. Me and him. He's my father, isn't he?'

'What of it?'

That's not what I want you to say. I'm your daughter too, remember? Ceri said, 'He might ask me to go to America with him.'

Sam dodged past on the far side of the room.

Mum stood where she was, staring at Ceri. Then she closed her eyes, as if she felt ill. 'If you do that you'll be making a big mistake.' Her voice was quiet, but uneven, as if she was trying to stay calm. She opened her eyes again.

Ceri looked away. 'Let me make it then. I'm old enough.'

'You are not,' Mum said. 'And you're not going.'

Ceri shouted inside her head. Never mind whether I'm going. Tell me you want me here. She jammed her lips tight over the words and glared at her mother. 'I can do what I like. Just you wait.'

Something in Ceri's look, or what she had said, or maybe just sheer exasperation, must have been the last straw. 'You have absolutely no idea,' her mother snapped. 'Remember – if you can – that when you make mistakes now, there's me to clear up the mess. But you won't get any wiser when you grow up. You'll carry on making mistakes and marry a psychopath like I did – '

'My father is not a psychopath!' Ceri shouted.

'So you tell me why he hit me over the head with a champagne bottle!' Mum shouted back.

There was a dreadful silence: and into it Sam asked, 'Was it full?'

'No of course it wasn't, there never were any full ones when Paul was around and anyway it was at the end of the party, what would you expect *and this is not funny*!' Mum yelled. Then she threw her mug of coffee across the room and ran out, slamming the door.

They watched the coffee trickling down the pale wall. Ceri fought down the panicky laughter that had risen to her lips when Sam asked his question, and went to pick up the mug. 'Miracle,' she said. 'Not broken.'

'But what did I say that was funny?' Sam asked her.

'Oh, I don't know. Only the way the first thing came into your head, was it full?' What Ceri did not say was, I never felt less like laughing.

Sam took the mug and swiped his finger round the inside of it. 'She's on the sugar again.' When Ceri fetched the dishcloth from the kitchen and began wiping the coffee from the wall, he said, 'You're only making it worse.'

'I don't believe it,' Ceri said.

'Well, you are. Look at it.'

'No. I don't believe he hit her.'

Sam licked the sugar from his finger. 'Mum doesn't tell lies.'

'But she doesn't see things the way we do. You know that.'

Sam snorted. 'How can she see being hit on the head in a way we wouldn't?'

'But he's not *like* that!'

'You'd say that, wouldn't you?' Sam said. 'What's so brilliant about him anyway?'

Ceri said, 'You should have been at the hotel. I felt really important, being with him. He made me feel important. That's what it is.'

'He's not my father,' Sam said.

'Shut up. Hughes.'

He glared at her. 'Be like that then. See if I care. Schaefer.' He slammed out of the room: and Ceri, standing with the wet dish-cloth in her hand, remembered the look her father had given her when he ordered the champagne.

She went up to her room again. Sam was there, his hand down the back of the bed, where she had hidden the seal skin. Ceri banged the open door against the wall and said, 'What do you think you're doing? Get out!'

Sam stood up. 'I want my stereo back.'

'On the floor. There. In front of your face. Go away.' Ceri clicked the door shut behind him, sat down on the bed, and hurled her hearing aids across the room. Anger had brought the tinnitus back, a hissing waterfall in her ears even when she jammed her fingers into them. After a moment she hit her ears twice, with her clenched fists, and buried her head under the pillow.

The house quivered slightly. A door opening, or closing? It might be Mum coming back, or Sam going out. Or the wind, blowing. Ceri sat up and brushed her hair out of her eyes. She walked to the door, and fumbled with the handle.

Fergal was standing on the landing. He said something.

'Come in,' Ceri said, and turned away from him to look for her hearing aids. They had fallen in the farthest, most awkward corner. Kneeling, putting them in, she had a brief glimpse in the mirror of Fergal looking at her, his face unreadable. 'Did you want something?' she asked.

'I left some books here last Christmas. Sorry to bother you and all that, but I've some reading to do for Sussex.'

'Christmas?' Ceri said, watching Fergal stretch for the top shelf. 'Stand on the bed if you want to.'

'Thanks.' He kicked his shoes off and climbed up. One book after another, small pale-covered paperbacks, thudded on the duvet. 'We stay with each other alternate Christmases. My parents; Uncle John and Aunt Morag; Mum's sister Jean and her family at Braemar.'

'Must be fun.'

'Tis.' Fergal stepped down to the floor again. 'My Braemar cousins get snowed out of school three days in five, wintertime. I used to be dead jealous.'

Ceri picked up one of the books and looked at the flyleaf. 'Who's A. MacInnes?'

'Alec, probably. My brother. Though it might be my cousin Alison.' He leaned over and looked at the writing. 'Alison. She had to do that for A-level. But Alec did French too. He'll have the farm some day, but he said that was no reason not to study something irrelevant while there was time.'

'And you said the Scots are a practical nation.'

'Well, so we are.'

Ceri laughed; and Fergal, sounding irritated beyond endurance, snapped, 'Don't *laugh* at me!'

'Sorry – sorry,' Ceri said, trying not to mumble. 'I didn't . . .'

Her voice trailed away. She didn't even know what she hadn't meant to do.

'I wish you'd – oh, never mind,' Fergal said, as if she hadn't spoken, and put his shoes on again.

'I owe you that money still,' Ceri said unhappily. She opened drawers and doors looking for her purse; and turning round with the notes in her fingers, had another glimpse of Fergal in the mirror: leaning over, his hands on the far edge of the bed, immobile, as if he had just had a shock.

'Fergal?'

He stood up abruptly. 'Sorry.'

'How much was it?'

'Oh . . . can't remember.' But he looked at what she was holding, and dug in his pockets for change. 'Here you are.'

'Would you – would you like some coffee?' Ceri asked. 'I think it'll still be hot.'

'Thanks,' Fergal said. 'Yes please.' He spoke in strange, bitten-off, sentences, as if there was another conversation somewhere that he was trying to hear.

'Fergal,' Ceri said. 'I'm sorry. I don't mean just now. But last night too. I was – cross.'

'You were a first class nuisance,' Fergal said. 'But I forgive you.' He looked at her face, and laughed. 'Okay, so I was rude too. Forgiving but frank Fergal, that's me. Alliterating your cares away.'

'You do talk rubbish. What's alliterating, anyway?'

'Alliteration. Much beloved by unpublished children's authors. Denny the dormouse. Ronnie the rabbit. Squiffy the squid. You get the idea.'

They sat facing each other across the kitchen table. Ceri's

mug of coffee had gone tepid, but Fergal's was hot from the percolator. He took a mouthful, reached for the books he had brought downstairs. 'This one's yours.'

It was Ceri's book of Scottish songs, mixed up in the pile. 'Have you got that?' she asked.

'No – I've better versions of most of those songs.'

'Is the Great Silkie one very different?'

'Oh, not so much,' Fergal said. 'This is what you might call an export version – the Scottishness gets watered down.'

'Ruth . . .' Ceri said slowly.

'What about her?'

'Don't laugh . . . you must know what I think about her and Euan . . . do you think she might be – under an enchantment?'

Fergal looked at her from under level brows. 'If you ask me,' he said, 'it's not Ruth that's under the enchantment.' He swallowed the rest of his coffee. 'I must go.' He went out by the seaward door, and stopped. After a moment he turned back to add, 'And I don't mean Euan either.'

'Who do you mean, then?' Ceri asked; but he would not answer. She followed him outside, and watched as he struggled to get his car keys from the pocket on the same side as the arm he was holding the books with. 'Can I help?'

Fergal shook his head; opened the door at last, leaned over to dump the books, and wriggled into the driver's seat. He didn't look back as he drove off, but then maybe he wouldn't have seen anything through the cloud of exhaust fumes.

Ceri wandered down to the foreshore, and kicked pebbles. There was the boulder she had been sitting on when Euan first spoke to her. Perhaps if she sat there again . . .

Euan didn't come, but after a while she saw Ruth, strolling

along the shore from the direction of her own cottage. Ceri waved. No response. She waved again.

This time Ruth saw her, and turned inland, trudging up the pebbly slope. 'Hiya,' she said when she was close enough. 'The oddest thing. You know that key I lost?'

'I remember.'

'It turned up again, yesterday. Someone must have pushed it through the mail slot, I found it on the floor.'

'Not me,' Ceri said.

'I never thought it was.'

'So do you want – it – back?' Ceri looked at Ruth narrowly. Does she actually know what it is, whose it is? If she does – will she tell me? She doesn't realise I've worked it out for myself . . . and if she doesn't know what it is, why is she hiding it?

'Uh . . .' Ruth said, 'no, you keep it. I'll get it back – oh, some time.' She looked at Ceri. 'What's up?'

'I had a row with Mum.'

Ruth laughed. 'Hey, what teenager never did?'

'It was because I went out with,' Ceri said, and as usual had to stop and organise the word, 'my father. I mean, our father.'

'Ah,' Ruth said. 'I get the problem.'

'He wants me to – that is, he asked me if I'd like to – go to America with him.' She waited for a response: there was none. 'What should I do?'

'Don't ask me,' Ruth said. 'I'm biased, remember? My mom wouldn't stick with him.'

'Um – why not?' Ceri asked.

Ruth grinned. 'He didn't like it when she got bigger than size 14. That would be size 16 in English, mind. Well – my mom has zest for life, which beats a neat figure any day, and she wasn't out to let him cramp her style. So she quit.'

'She sounds nice.'

'She's great. She persuaded me to come over here.' Ruth sighed. 'I guess I owe her a lot. Indirectly. Euan and all that. But it hasn't worked.'

'What hasn't?'

Ruth looked embarrassed. 'I hate the ocean. I get afraid of it. I always did. Mom thought a dose of working on an island might cure me, and she was kind of hooked on Scotland.'

'But you still hate the sea,' Ceri said.

'Yep,' Ruth said briskly: and then, so quietly that Ceri wasn't sure even if she'd read her lips correctly, 'And I'm not sharing Euan with anything.'

Anything? Ceri thought. Anyone? What am I doing? How do I dare think – . She swallowed. Maybe I didn't get it right, what she said.

Liar.

Ruth stood up suddenly. 'I must go. Look, don't worry too much about your mom. She loves you and she hates him. Hardly surprising if she gets mad now and again.'

'But what am I going to *do*?'

Ruth looked at her. 'Remember what I told you. Think real hard. About everything.' And then she was on her way.

It wasn't so easy to think. Mum was in her worst mood that evening, nag nag nag even at Sam. Ceri went to bed before she really wanted to. 'Night, Mum.'

If there was an answer Mum didn't turn round to give it.

It was black night, starless under the cloud. Ceri pulled the seal skin from its hiding place and tried to think herself into her undersea country; but all she could see in her mind was Mum's face, screwed up with rage, and Sam's, stony with anger. They don't care what I want. They don't care. Tears trickled out of the sides of Ceri's eyes. Even Ruth won't help. And now I can't get out. She tried again, but the undersea country was as distant as if she had never imagined it. Ceri turned so that she lay alongside the seal skin, and licked the salt from her face, where the tears had run in at the corner of her mouth. If she could not cut loose from the world of sound, then sleep and dreams would be her only escape. If she could sleep at all.

She wandered outside under the clouds. The turf prickled her toes with a tiny sharp feel like pins and needles. From the grass to the narrow margin of sand, from the sand to the crunching shingle. In her hand something soft and warm. Ceri wrapped it round her and walked on, not stopping for the edge of the sea where the blackness shone faintly, even under this dark sky.

The water had its own voice, not of sound but of touch, pressing her round with a hundred fingertips of wave and tide and current. She began to swim. The waves were boisterous, they bounced past irresistibly, until she could leap them like hurdles. Time stretched, as it does in dreams; and then Ceri saw movement. It wasn't hard to see in the dark, but she couldn't focus: when she did, she saw – Euan, running to the sea in a pent-up fury that seemed to explode into speed. Her dream-eyes showed Ceri a cloud of anger round him, but her ears told her nothing. An unreasoned fear took hold of her. She flipped over and began to swim again, as fast as she could.

Out of the water at last, a few moments stumbling on the pebbles – how clumsy her legs were! – and up, her feet dragging over the ground. Inside the house. She turned and saw through the open door, the seaward door, Euan standing outside, unmoving behind a barrier invisible as glass.

Thirteen

Ceri sat up. Her heart was thumping. It was still dark. She rolled awkwardly out of bed and crossed the floor. Fumbling the curtain aside, she looked out of the window at the loch, a hardly-seen flicker of moving water. There was nobody outside. Of course there was nobody there. Least of all Euan. She opened the window and leaned out. Through the not-quite-silence of her ears pushed another sound, a humming or singing that might have come from a human throat – if there had been anyone there. Ceri shivered, and closed the window.

She rose out of more dreams in which she knew she had visited her undersea country, but as she woke it slipped out of her mind, and could not be remembered. She lay for a while, eyes open, staring at the pillow in front of her face. The house was still, not a twang or thump of movement in the boards anywhere. It must be very early.

Last night she had left the curtains a little open, and now she could see a slit of the outside world stacked with layers of land, sea, sky. Ceri went to sit on the floor by the window, with the seal skin wrapped round her toes to keep them warm. The shadow of the hills stretched across the house to the water's edge and beyond. There was no wind, hardly a ripple, only a slow, silky swell that was difficult to watch. Farther out, the early sunlight had reached the sea beyond the loch, and farther away still an island floated like a shadow on the horizon.

From behind the rocky point came a ripple, and then Euan's dinghy, with Euan himself sitting hunched at the oars. He was rowing half-heartedly, one stroke at a time, and then letting the dinghy drift. As Ceri watched, he shipped the oars completely, bowed his head, and rested his face on his folded arms. The ripples of his rowing died away.

There were more ripples. The dinghy seemed to shift on the water, and Euan sat up with a jolt. With a thrill of excitement Ceri saw that there were seals crowding all around him. Euan leaned over the gunwale and held out his hands. Even at that distance Ceri could see how taut his arms were stretched as he dipped them into the water, touching the dark heads that jostled round him like Hallowe'en apples; moving bit by bit out of his reach. Something had to happen: and at last it did. Euan, leaning farther and farther out, shifted his foothold, and upset the balance of the dinghy. It flicked sideways, tipped him out into the water, and rocked back to an even keel.

For a moment Euan disappeared completely. Ceri leapt to her feet and pressed herself against the window, clutching the seal skin to herself. The sun lifted above the hills behind the house, and the creatures in the water glittered with moving light. Euan shot out into the air as if someone had boosted him, turned and dived back down neatly as a dolphin. It was like the time before, when he had swum with the seals, but wilder, fiercer, as if he knew there was nobody to see them. And then at last Euan, flinging his head back and pushing his wet hair out of his eyes, looked straight at the gap in the curtain and saw Ceri standing there with the seal skin clutched between her hands.

She knew he had seen her. Nothing else could explain how still he was. Ceri's breath began to come fast and shallow. The fixity of Euan's gaze seemed to rock her on her feet, but she could not move. Then Euan, leaving the dinghy to drift, began swimming for the shore, fast hard strokes that dragged at the water. Ceri snatched the curtains shut, stared at the thing between her hands, and turned in a panic towards the bed. Under the mattress. She pushed it as far as she could reach, sobbing for breath, fear as unreasoned as the night's dream tightening her throat and chest. She dragged some clothes on, trainers, snapped a lace and knotted it and tied it again. If Euan found her in the house he would ask questions she would have to answer. She would not be able to keep Ruth's secret or her own. Ceri whisked out of the inland door and fled.

Running so fast: it seemed she could hardly feel the ground beneath her feet. Ceri leapt a tussock of grass. She was at the crest of the slope down to Ruth's cottage. Something flashed in her eyes. A car on the other side of the hollow. The headlights flicked at her again, and she recognised the colour, quite unmistakeable. Ceri changed direction.

Fergal opened the door, and was halfway out of the clockwork marshmallow as she came up the slope towards him. 'Something wrong? Come to Aunt Morag's with me, she'll be out at the milking. Ruth won't be awake yet.'

'Y – no.' Ceri stopped, breathing hard. 'Nothing wrong.'

'No? Taken up jogging, then?'

'I – ' Ceri leaned against the car. 'Didn't want to meet Euan. Ran out of the house.'

Fergal raised one eyebrow; but all he said was, 'Euan doesn't come indoors unless invited. Had you not noticed?'

'Now you remind me, yes,' Ceri said. 'Yes.' She sat down where she was. 'My knees are shaking.' She had to crick her neck to look at Fergal's lips.

'You are a strange one,' Fergal said. 'All this stramash.' (What did *that* mean?) 'And for why?'

'Can't tell you.'

'Mm.' Fergal didn't look convinced. 'Shall I give you a lift back?'

'Thanks. Rather go for a walk.'

Fergal swung his legs back into the car. 'Won't your mother be sending out search parties if you're not at breakfast?'

'Tell your aunt to tell her I'm OK.' Ceri stood up and shut the door for him. Fergal wound the window down. 'You were going to your aunt?'

'I was that. Are you sure?'

'Quite sure.'

Fergal's reply was lost in the roar of the engine as he drove off. Ceri walked aimlessly in a small circle. Oh, what now? She was facing Ruth's cottage. A whisk of movement at a window – pulling the curtains back. With a sigh Ceri set off down the slope, trying to straighten the words inside her head that would tell Ruth what had happened.

'He can't have seen you,' Ruth said. 'Not from that distance.' She was brushing her hair, tugging the brush through it until the fine threads blew like soft flame round her shoulders.

146

'He must have. Or why did he – come ashore?' Ceri bit her tongue back from telling Ruth that Euan had been swimming with the seals. Somewhere between Ruth and Euan there was a promise, she knew that much; somewhere between Euan and Ceri there was a secret that she couldn't quite catch or identify, slipping through her mind like water. And now Ceri wasn't quite sure why she had come running to Ruth. 'I'm sure he knows,' she said.

Ruth bit her lip and said, 'Bring it back here then. I'll lock it in the cupboard.'

'Ruth,' Ceri said.

'Mm?'

'Why don't you just give it back to him?'

'I – he – how do you know it's his?' Ruth said.

'You just told me, for one thing.'

Ruth missed her stroke, and the brush clattered to the floor. 'You haven't been – you can't have, you *can't . . .*' Her words disappeared with her lips as her hair swung across her face.

Ceri handed the brush back to her. 'Swimming? No. I just – guessed.'

Ruth stared at the brush as if she didn't know what it was for. 'I thought I'd been so careful.'

'I heard the song about it. And read the words. Things Euan said, too.'

'Tell me I'm not crazy,' Ruth said. 'Tell me I'm not imagining things. Tell me Euan is – just like anyone else.'

'We can't both be crazy. Euan never would be like anyone else,' said Ceri.

Ruth smiled. 'No. He would not. I guess it has to be real. And if it is – I don't want the sea to have him.'

A sudden jealousy thumped in Ceri's heart, so hard that she turned her face away from Ruth, in case it showed there. This is my sister, what am I doing? And – the sea is my country, she thought. What if – ? 'Maybe we don't need to worry after all, if he won't come in the house,' she said. Oh, this is dreadful. We can't both – I can't ...

'Well. I guess not,' Ruth said doubtfully. 'I gave him a standing invitation to this place. He might be in and out any time.' She looked Ceri in the eyes. 'What are we doing? You and me. Believing the impossible.'

Ceri said, 'Suits me.'

'Oh sure . . . you and your unicorns.'

Ceri smiled. What she felt like saying was, I've changed, Ruth, haven't you noticed? Instead, she said, 'I ought to go back. Let me know . . .'

'Know what?' Ruth asked.

'If anything happens.'

Ruth nodded, and followed her to the door without saying anything. At the top of the slope Ceri turned and waved; Ruth, shaking the table-cloth out of the front door, caught it up in one hand and blew her a kiss. Ceri walked back to house trying to believe the impossible; or to ignore the real, she wasn't quite sure which. Ruth and Euan . . .

Breakfast was an uncomfortable meal. Ceri had always admitted to herself that one of Mum's best points was her refusal to drag arguments over from one day to the next; but this morning that was obviously proving difficult. Between seeing Euan and Fergal and Ruth, she herself had almost forgotten the intensity of last night's argument; but Mum had black shadows under her eyes, and was forgetting to smile.

It was Sam and Ceri's turn to wash up, and even that went by silently, for Ceri at any rate: Sam had his personal stereo in, and marked a phantom beat with the tea-towel. When Ceri came through the lounge to go upstairs, Mum was sitting in the corner with one hand to her lips. Ceri almost expected to smell cigarette smoke. She took a deep breath. 'May I go swimming?'

'If Mr and Mrs MacInnes say it's safe, yes,' her mother said, not looking up, but moving her hand away from her lips.

'Thanks,' Ceri said, and took the stairs two at a time. She rummaged for her swimsuit, flung it on the bed, and then remembered what lay under the mattress. Dare I – ? No. Yes. It's Euan's. But. This may be my only chance. I could swim with it . . . she slid her hand under the edge of the mattress.

Nothing there. 'There must be,' Ceri said aloud, and heaved at the mattress, lifting it clear of the bed. Maybe I pushed it too far, and it fell out on the other side. She let the mattress drop, and lay flat on the floor to look under the bed. Nothing there. Wedged against the wall, then. She pulled the bed towards her and hung head-down over the far side. Still nothing there. Three times makes it true, and now I know what they mean when they talk about hearts sinking. Frantically Ceri shook out the duvet, the pillows, even the clothes she had worn yesterday. Nothing, nothing, nothing. She turned round, and there in the doorway was Sam.

'What are you doing?' they said to each other.

'Nothing.'

'Oh, come on,' Sam said. 'You don't crash round the room like that for nothing.'

'*You've* got it,' Ceri said.

'What do you mean? I haven't been in your room.'

'Liar,' Ceri said. 'You're the only one who knows it's here except Ruth.' And Euan, she reminded herself, only he hasn't been invited in. 'Did Euan come in?'

'You call *me* a liar?' Sam snapped. 'What about yourself? And I haven't seen your precious Euan for days, and I still don't know what you're looking for.'

'The seal skin. The one Ruth gave me.'

Sam's face changed. 'So you have got it,' Ceri said.

'I have not!' Sam added defensively, 'I knew what it was, 'course, when I saw it that time. But I did not take it. Not not *not*.'

'Where is it, then?' Ceri cried. 'Because it's not here.'

'Oh, I don't know and I don't care,' Sam said. 'We're supposed to be on holiday, for heaven's sake. I might enjoy myself if it wasn't for you shouting around like something out of a soap-opera.'

'Well, I've a bloody good reason to shout, haven't I?' Ceri snapped. Sam turned round, muttering something under his breath, and slammed out of the room. Ceri walked desperately to the window and leant her forehead against the cool glass. I was always on good terms with Sam before, what's come over me, what's come over him? It has to have been Sam, who else can it be? And Mum won't listen to me probably after I went out with Dad, and how do I tell Ruth it's missing? And Euan? Her mouth opened and she said 'Euan' before she could stop herself.

What's happening to me?

It felt as if the world was coming apart. The wind blew around the house like echoes of anger: if she went out of the house that would be all she would hear.

In the evening, when the sunlight on the gorse and heather was so bright it almost hurt to look at, she went down to the beach. The wind snatched the door out of her hand, and buffeted her along the path.

Euan was waiting for her. She saw him standing with his back to her, looking along the loch and out to sea. As soon as she came to the edge of the shingle he turned, as if he knew she was there, and stood, quite still, watching her while she walked down. Ceri's heart began to thump, her mouth dried. I can't be afraid of Euan. I can't. But I wish he'd say something.

He said nothing when she reached him; only looked at her for a long moment, turned his back on her again, and walked away. Ceri followed him.

Euan was making for the headland where Ruth said he lived, walking fast, easily barefoot even over the stones and rough ground. When Ceri stopped, out of breath, he merely paused in his stride, waited until she was ready, and went on again.

The house on the headland was a ruin; in the single tree that had once sheltered it from the wind there was a bird's nest, a ragged crazy affair of twigs that looked as if the next gale would send it flying. Euan waited at the doorway, ushered Ceri in with an ironic, silent bow, and stepped over the threshold. There was no door to close, and the wind blew through the room coldly as fear. Ceri looked at Euan: she could neither look away from him, nor speak.

'Well?' His voice was dry, quiet, almost unrecognisable.

'What do you want?'

'Where is it?'

She swallowed. 'Where is what?'

'You know,' he said, his voice not changing. 'You know what I mean.'

'The – ' Even now, her tongue stumbled over the unlikeliness of the words, the impossibility of what it must all mean. 'The seal skin?'

'Yes.' Over their heads the wind made a cold blue ceiling of air. Ceri said, 'It is yours, then.'

Euan said, 'It is. I am a man upon the land . . .' His voice faded into silence.

'And you did see me this morning.'

'Not just this morning,' Euan said. 'Last night.'

Ceri closed her eyes briefly as the memory of the spinning water hit her again. 'But I was dreaming!' she said, and stopped, aghast, her heart thumping in her chest. Euan shook his head.

She scrabbled for words. 'Not me,' she protested, 'it can't . . .'

Euan stood like a rock, like a stone wall. 'It did. You were like me. A silkie in the sea.'

'It's not true!' Ceri cried. Even now, even against all the times before when she had persuaded herself it was true. If only.

Euan's face twitched; he nodded, as if he had picked up a signal on a secret wavelength. 'It is,' he said. 'It's true and you know it.' Two strides forward, and he put his hands on her shoulders and shook her. 'This is not a game. *Don't deceive me*!'

'I know,' Ceri said breathlessly. 'Not a game. I like it real—'

Euan jerked his head back and looked at her. 'Aren't you afraid of the sea?' he asked strangely. His hands were still on her shoulders.

Ceri said, 'Never.'

'Ruth is,' he said.

Without quite knowing what words she spoke, Ceri said, 'I could never be afraid of you.'

Euan made a strange noise in the back of his throat, and came closer. Ceri smelt the salt and seaweed tang of the sea on his skin; it was as warm as if there was a fire under it. Like the seal she had touched. She closed her eyes and leaned on him, and his arms went round her.

Then with a sudden indrawn breath he pulled away. 'But where *is* it?' Ceri stumbled forward, and he caught her arms; the words were dragged out of her mouth as he let go of her. 'Someone stole it. Out of my room.'

Euan flung back his head and let out what would have been a yell, if something had not changed it into a dry and strangled sound of agony: then he stood there, breathing hard, and it seemed to Ceri that she could see all his skin flickering with anger. 'Who?'

'I don't know.' She stood irresolute. Euan stared at her as he had done earlier, impersonal as the wind above their heads. He said, 'When you do – promise you'll tell me.'

Ceri peeled her lips open. They were so dry. 'I can't promise,' she said.

'Why?'

'In case . . .' She could not tell him. 'In case . . .' She dragged the words out. 'I can wear it again.' Somewhere to belong; her undersea land . . .

Euan said, 'It's mine.' That strange fierce look she had seen before on his face when he was angry: he stepped forward and put his hands on her shoulders again. 'You don't understand.

When it was in the water – I knew. Burn it, bury it, drown it – *I'll know*. It's part of me.'

Ceri said, 'I've worn it—'

'Would you want to be one of us?' Euan demanded. His gaze locked into hers. She stared back at him. Silence. And then Euan kissed her.

Ceri did not have enough breath to draw in. It was unlike anything she had expected; like being caught under a thunderstorm, a falling wave. She was drowning, she had to breathe. She pulled her head away. 'Euan!'

He let go of her and stepped back. 'Remember!' he said. Then he turned and ran through the doorway. With her hand to her lips Ceri walked out of the door and watched him; he slithered and jumped down to the beach and made direct for the sea. But when he reached the sea he did not go in. Instead he ran along the beach, desperately, like a hunted man, veering towards the water and then sharply away from it, as if the line of foam at the water's edge fizzed and sparkled with an electric current, keeping him away from sanctuary. Soon he was out of sight.

Fourteen

Ceri closed her eyes. She felt sick. What happens next, what happens now? The world is turning round under my feet. But then it always does, round and round on its axis twenty-four hours a day, whirling round the sun, and the sun through the galaxy and . . . she swallowed, trying to put the universe out of her mind. Concentrate on something small. At her feet was a tiny spiral shell; she bent and picked it up. Such intricate perfect detail. She had seen a model of the human ear once, like the inside of a shell. Some people said you could hear the sound of the sea if you put a shell to your ear: but her own ears did it for Ceri, without the need for sea-shells.

She put the shell into her pocket, and stepped forward. The beach was not so very close. How big a storm had there been to fling the shell up from the sea to rest here, on the threshold of Euan's cottage? Ceri looked down at the beach. The tide must be just turning from the ebb: scraps of weed and driftwood were being carried higher up the shingle with each wave. She picked her way down to the beach the way Euan had gone, and wandered home along the tide's edge.

Next morning when she put her hearing aids in and went to flick the switch, she found that she hadn't turned them off the night before. Ceri twiddled the volume control, but the world's noise didn't change. She took the aids out, and put her head round the door of Sam's room.

'Sam, where's Mum?'

Sam looked aside, the way Ceri did when she didn't want to listen. 'I said,' she began, gave up, and followed the smell of coffee downstairs.

'My batteries are flat.'

'Didn't you send the book off for some more?' Mum said, putting down a dried plate and twisting the tea-towel between her hands. 'I told you to, when you changed the last one.'

'Yes.'

Mum looked faintly exasperated. 'So when did you post it?'

Ceri shrugged. 'Can't remember. Anyway it didn't come back before we went away.'

Something made Mum look at her, and then say, 'I suppose you did it on purpose.'

'You know I hate them.' Ceri stalked across the kitchen and kicked the fridge door. '*Hate* them. Roaring and howling in my ears and blotting out what I really want to listen to.' She knew she was exaggerating, but a real excuse to lose her temper was welcome. 'Why should I walk around with them in my ears just to make life easier for you?'

'It's not about making life easy,' her mother retorted. 'It's about communicating.'

'So what?'

'So it takes two, for a start,' her mother said. 'What's the point of speaking up if you won't listen to us?'

'And what's the point of listening, when you don't say anything worth hearing?'

Her mother cracked the tea-towel against the work-surface, like a whip. 'You are just trying to make life difficult!'

'You said it wasn't about making life easy,' Ceri reminded her.

'Okay, okay,' her mother said, sounding suddenly and uncannily American. 'You keep listening. Maybe I'll say something you'll condescend to be interested in. Eventually.'

Ceri couldn't help it: she had to grin. But couldn't give in that easily. 'Will you let me go to sign language classes, then?'

'Oh, Ceri – I've told you before you don't need to.'

'I might not need to learn Esperanto either, but I bet you'd let me go to that.'

It was her mother's turn to grin. 'Your point. Advantage Miss Schaefer. All right, you can go. Though you might be too old now to learn it really well.'

'Deuce,' said Ceri. 'But just you watch me try. Anything else?' *What am I doing arranging sign language classes? I might be going to America.*

'You might try making it up with Sam,' Mum said.

'How can I? You tell him – ' Ceri stopped. 'Has he told you what it's about?'

'No.'

'Something's missing from my room. And only he can have taken it.'

Her mother frowned. 'Not like Sam . . . is it valuable? What is it?'

'Well . . .' Ceri found she did not want to tell her mother

exactly what it was. 'Not money, or anything like that. Nothing he could sell.' Could you sell a seal skin? It was probably another thing you needed a licence for. 'But special. And not actually mine.'

'So how did you get hold of it?' her mother asked with raised eyebrows.

'From Ruth. To look after.' Ceri scuffed her toes along the bottom of the fridge, feeling the vibration from the textured surround quiver up her leg. She didn't hear the next thing her mother said. 'Sorry?'

'I said, I'll have a word with Sam.'

'Thanks.' Ceri decided to skip breakfast. A cup of coffee would do. She took it out on to the lawn, and stood with her nose over the cup, absorbing the smell, and feeling the steam condense on her skin. Why did coffee never taste quite as good as it smelt?

Something made her look up. There on the line between grass and shingle was Euan. He was dripping wet, like a drowned man. A long dark-red ribbon of seaweed was caught round his neck; as if his throat had been cut. Ceri backed off before she could stop herself. Euan stood watching as she retreated into the house and closed the door between herself and him.

Mum and Sam were still eating breakfast, and the world came whirling back to normal. Ceri sat quietly beside them, answering Mum's questions at random, and somehow managing to say no when invited out shopping. When Mum and Sam had clattered out of the inland door she went upstairs. Euan was nowhere to be seen. But he must be out there, some-where, anywhere. Waiting for her.

All the long morning Ceri stayed indoors. She tried painting, whale-song, day-dreaming, but nothing could quieten her thoughts. At last she picked up the telephone and dialled The Shieling's number. The voice at the other end was horribly faint now she didn't have her hearing aids in, and she could only just hear her father's extension ringing. Fourteen times, plus three, plus one for luck. She put the receiver down, then tried the switchboard again.

'If my father comes in, will you ask him to call me?'

'Certainly, Miss Schaefer. What number was it?'

After that she stretched the telephone cord to its utmost so that she could sit on the sofa with the phone beside her, and channel-hopped on the television. Thank heavens for foreign films with subtitles.

But all she could find was something Spanish about death, and that was hard enough to understand even with subtitles. Ceri was wondering whether a soap-opera was predictable enough to follow if you couldn't hear the words, when the phone rang.

'Dad?' She crammed the receiver against her ear.

'Hi, Ceri. You called?'

She could hear him – just. 'I want to talk to you. Can you come round this evening?'

'Sure. Like to talk to you myself,' her father said. 'What time?'

'Seven? Eight?'

'Half after seven. I'll see you.'

'Okay, Dad. Thanks.' Ceri put the receiver down and carried the phone back into the kitchen. As soon as she sat down again, Mum and Sam came back.

Mum dropped something on to her lap. 'Here.'

A pack of zinc batteries. 'How did you get these?'

'Bit of special pleading in the health centre,' her mother said. 'What have you been doing with yourself?'

'Watching television.' Ceri glanced at the screen, where the Spanish film was winding itself up in a cocoon of gloom. 'Might as well turn it off really.'

'I talked to Sam,' her mother said. 'He says he hasn't taken anything from your room.'

'He'd say that, wouldn't he?'

'And I believe him.'

'Oh.' Ceri looked at her mother. 'But – '

'I said, I believe him. There are no buts.'

Ceri pressed her lips together, and took up her wooden seal. 'I asked Dad to come here tonight. I want to talk to him.'

Her mother took a deep, sharp breath, like someone about to lose her temper. Then the breath went out in a long sigh. 'All right. But I hope you're not expecting me to be here.'

'Well – no. But what else can you do?'

'I'll take Sam out to the cinema at Fort William. I suppose that means we'll miss the last ferry at Corran.'

'Will you be stuck?'

Mum shook her head. 'We'll have to come back the long way round, that's all. Round the head of the loch and through Glenfinnan.'

'Thanks.'

'Anything,' her mother said.

'What?'

'To keep away from Paul.'

Ceri got to her feet, stamped, and went upstairs without

160

looking back. You're talking about my father, remember? She fingered the packet of batteries, then took one out and peeled the cover off. I suppose it's a good thing I've got these, if I'm going to be talking to him.

Paul was very prompt. Ceri had thought of asking Morag MacInnes if she had any whisky, for him to drink: but in the end she just made coffee, and it was percolating when he arrived. They sat side by side on the sofa, her father with his free arm along the back. Ceri had pulled the blind half-down over the picture window, and the sunshine that would have slanted dazzling into the room was transmuted into a greenish underwater light.

'So what did you want to talk about?' Paul asked.

'Don't know, really,' she said. 'I just wanted to see you again. Does that sound stupid?'

'Would I say so?' He looked down at her. 'You got something else on your mind? You look kind of hassled.'

Ceri shook her head, but said, 'Mum keeps – she just isn't the sort you can talk to about important things.' She bit her lip. That isn't entirely true. You know it.

But it's always her own point of view she gives.

And why shouldn't it be?

'Hey,' Paul said, 'if a girl can't tell her father, who can she tell? I'm here; try me.'

'If I want something different,' Ceri burst out, 'she thinks I'm getting at her for having things the way they are. I do want someone else – if I talk to myself I just get confused.'

'What about Sam?'

'He's not talking to me. We had a row.'

'Tough luck,' Paul said sympathetically, and dropped his arm so that it lay across her shoulders. 'Wish I could help out.'

'Shouldn't think he'd listen to you,' Ceri said.

'Oh, I don't know.' Her father sounded almost as if she had made him a dare. Ceri glanced at his face and saw a look of – confidence? determination? on it that she could not quite decipher. He smiled at her and said, 'You make good coffee.'

'I do? Thanks.' Ceri took a sip from her own mug. 'What was it you wanted to talk about?'

'Uh – beside you and your brilliant coffee?' He paused. 'Ruth, I guess. You see her much?'

'Not that much.'

Her father shook his head. 'No, I meant this vacation. Have you been going round with her?'

'Oh – I've been to her cottage. Had a picnic. One or two other times.'

'She wrote me about some guy she met. Did you meet him?'

Ceri blinked. It wasn't easy to think of Euan as just some guy you met. 'Yes,' she said.

'What do you know about him?' Paul asked.

'Nothing,' Ceri said. The word rang inside her head. All my lies say 'nothing'. Perhaps nothing will come back to haunt me.

Paul grunted. 'Is he aiming to marry her? Has he got money?'

'He never seems to need money. About Ruth – I don't know.' Ceri felt her fingertips touch her mouth, though she hadn't meant to move her hand. She could not imagine Euan being married. Or was it just that she didn't want to? 'I don't know what Ruth wants to do,' she said, aware that this did not answer the question.

162

She felt Paul's fingers tighten briefly on her shoulder. 'And what do you want, Ceri kid?'

'Don't know that either. Not so as to tell you.' Ceri looked at him. 'I don't – ' She stopped.

'Don't what?' her father asked, smiling.

'Sam's nothing to do with you.'

'Maybe not. But you are.' He turned his head lazily to look at her. 'I want you to be happy.'

'I don't actually like not getting on with Sam,' she said.

'I'll have a talk with him, then. Whether he'll listen to me or not.'

'Don't lose your temper.'

'Do me credit, kid,' he said. 'Boys are the same everywhere. I'll get along just fine with him.'

Ceri nodded, but said nothing. After a little while her father looked at her again. 'Something else bothering you?'

She drew a quick breath. 'Mum says you hit her once.'

'Oh? And when does she say that was?'

'With a champagne bottle,' Ceri said. 'She didn't say when exactly.'

'Oh, that,' Paul said, and laughed uncomfortably. He moved his arm from around Ceri's shoulders. After a moment she noticed that he was holding his hands as she had seen them the first time they met, the fingers of his left hand cupped round his right wrist. He said, 'It was after a party, some dumb row we got into. Did she tell you she broke my wrist the same evening?'

'She did not!' Ceri said.

'Maybe I'd had a bit too much,' her father said. 'Yep, I guess I was a bit drunk. But so was Jen, and she was needling me. I mean, real needling. You ever lose your temper?'

'Sometimes. I scream and shout and stamp.'

'Attagirl.' Her father laughed. 'Jen goes kind of vicious. Or she used to. Well, so maybe I did take a swipe at her with a bottle. It was the first thing I could reach. Next I know she's grabbed it off me and hit back.'

'Mum?' Ceri said incredulously.

'Your mother. Yep.' He rubbed his wrist again. 'It sure hurt.'

'Not surprised,' Ceri said. What else could she say? How had she managed to have parents like this? She looked at her father. 'You wouldn't ever hit me. Would you?'

Her father threw his head back and laughed. 'Need you ask? Never. Never.'

Ceri was going to say something else, but at that moment a shadow flickered on the blind. She shot to her feet and looked through the edge of the window.

'Who is it?' her father said, coming to stand beside her.

'Euan.' Ceri felt her voice wobble.

He tugged at the cord, and the blind snapped into its rolled-up position. Ceri put her hand up to keep the sun out of her eyes. Euan was there, outside on the lawn, walking away from the window. He looked at them both for a long moment, turned away, and went down to the water's edge. There he began that intent, purposeful stride along the tideline that Ceri had seen before.

Her father said, 'That's him? He's this guy of Ruth's?'

She nodded.

'What kind of a hobo is he? I've seen him, he crews a boat round here.' Her father laughed shortly. 'I met him. He won't go far. Him!' He flung round from the window. 'She could have anything I can get her – anyone – and she goes for that.' He looked at Ceri. 'You said you met him. You like him?'

Ceri opened her mouth to answer, but what came out was, 'He kissed me.' Oh I didn't mean to tell him that, why did I say that?

'Did he heck?' her father said grimly. 'You sure moved fast when you saw that shadow . . .' He stopped suddenly, looked at her face, and put his hands on her shoulders. 'Ceri,' he said. 'Did he frighten you?'

'I,' she said. The memory of it flooded over her. She said nothing, only put her hand to her mouth again. Her father hugged her. 'Don't you worry about him,' he said. 'When you come to the States he'll be half the world away.'

'If.'

'Aw, come on!' he said, laughing, and hugged her again. 'Come with me. You know you'll love it.'

Ceri leaned against him, partly because he had pulled her off balance, partly because it was so nice, this feeling he gave her, of caring what happened, of wanting her to be happy. I'm sure Mum does but she won't say it. He makes all the difference, saying so. 'Guess I will,' she said. 'Oh, Dad . . . thanks for coming.'

'Thanks, nothing. And I'll call again tomorrow and chat to this Sam of yours. It'll be all right, you'll see.'

'I hope so.' She sighed. 'Be nice if someone else could sort it out.'

He looked down and smiled. 'You call me whenever you need me, okay? But right now I have to go. There are clients coming to the hotel for drinks in half an hour.'

'Big business,' Ceri said, teasing him.

'Sure is. Coming out to the car?'

'Course.'

The lounge seemed peculiarly empty when she was alone in it. At last Ceri gave up and went to bed. It seemed to be the only way she could stop thinking.

Fifteen

Sam went across to the MacInneses' farm after lunch the next day, and not much later Ceri saw him with John MacInnes climbing the slope behind the farm. They were away for a couple of hours, and either her father was watching from somewhere, or else he timed his arrival with uncanny precision. The sleek black car rolled up the track just as they re-appeared over the crest of the hill.

John MacInnes broke the air-gun open, took out the pellets, and leaned it against the wall. 'You're improving, Sam.'

Sam grinned. 'Like, I miss by one metre instead of by two?' John MacInnes laughed, pocketed the ammunition, and went out, waiting briefly by the door to let Ceri's father come in.

'Why did he leave that here?' Ceri demanded. It was difficult to ask it casually. She was still so certain that only Sam could have taken the seal skin from her room. And why had he done that, except to be as annoying as possible?

'Said I could clean it for him,' Sam told her.

'Nice gun,' Ceri's father said. 'You a good shot?'

'Mr MacInnes says I'm getting better,' Sam answered stiffly.

Paul leaned against the table and smiled. 'Well, that's not so bad.'

Ceri slipped out of the kitchen and sat at the other end of the lounge, where she could only hear their talk as a dim murmur. Presently her father came in.

'Okay?' she asked.

'Who knows? I did my best.' He smiled. 'Only the best for my daughter, remember?'

'I do,' she said. 'Thanks, Dad. See you soon.'

'You sure will.' He bent down, kissed her and went out again, upstairs and through the inland door. Like an echo of that door closing came the sound of the other door, the seaward door, opening, and then Mum's voice. Ceri went upstairs and put 'Chansons secrets des baleines' into her cassette player.

About ten minutes later Sam came straight in and switched the machine off.

'You're really trying to keep me down, aren't you?' he said. 'First you let on to Mum you don't trust me, and then you rope him in to try and make friends. I'm sticking to my own father, thank you.'

'I didn't mean it like that,' Ceri said helplessly. 'Honest I didn't.'

'How can you be so dim?' Sam demanded.

'Oh, thanks a lot. And what exactly do you mean?' Ceri kicked the table viciously. 'I suppose you believe everything Mum says about him.' Her feelings seemed to be trapped on a carousel – round and round, making her sick and dizzy.

'I said you were dim, and that proves it.' Then Sam added unexpectedly, 'I do get your point. About feeling important.

Maybe I would too if he was my father. But he's not. And I don't like him.'

'Fair enough. You're out to annoy me, you might as well hate my father.'

'I am not so! I just wish you'd behave like a normal sister sometimes.'

Normal? What does he mean, normal? The old resentment, of how Sam took his easy hearing for granted . . . the carousel took another spin. 'Suppose you'd like me to have normal hearing while you're about it!' Ceri snapped. 'Tough.'

'Oh, stop trying to make me feel sorry for you.'

Ceri opened her mouth: but just at that moment Mum ran upstairs and in at the bedroom door.

'Sam – John MacInnes outside. He forgot to arrange about tomorrow.'

'He taking you out with that gun again?' Ceri demanded.

'Yes. And why not? We need lunch.' Sam sighted along his outstretched arm. 'Perhaps I'll take a pot-shot at a seal.'

'If you do, I won't speak to you. Ever,' Ceri said coldly.

'That might be just as well, considering,' Sam retorted.

'Don't be ridiculous,' Mum said. 'Both of you. Mr MacInnes would never give his permission, for a start.'

Ceri recovered herself and said, 'Even if he did Sam would still be breaking the law.'

'Oh, stop behaving as if I was some kind of criminal,' Sam said furiously. 'Why do you always think I mean what I say?'

'How can I tell?' Ceri said. 'Nobody even says what they mean in this bloody family.'

'Ceri!' Mum said.

'Oh come *on*,' Ceri snapped. 'Don't pretend you never

swear. You used to drink and you used to smoke; *I* know. Dad told me how you broke his wrist. And you pretend you're so virtuous.'

Mum took two short strides towards Ceri with her arm raised. Then she stopped as abruptly as if she had walked into a brick wall. 'I am *not* going to descend to his level. Come on Sam. Arrange tomorrow with John and then we'll go out for another walk. We can get some peace and quiet that way.'

'Don't bother,' Ceri said. 'I'll go out for a change. Anything not to have to have you two yackety-yack round me all the time.' She put on her trainers and left the house, banging the door as hard as possible, trying to outrun the carousel in her head. I'll go where the road runs along by the sea. Where I met my father. She blinked the tears out of her eyes. The sun's so bright.

It would have been warm enough in the sun, but Ceri did not go right out on the beach and sit on the boulder where she had waited for Paul. She found herself a niche in the shelter of a dark crag that jutted out from the hillside. Nothing came along the road for a long time, but somehow she was not surprised when the first car she saw turned out to be shocking pink.

'What's up?' Fergal dropped down beside her, and linked his fingers round his knees.

'What are you doing here?'

'Aunt Morag said she saw you walking this way. So I thought I'd bring the car round in case you wanted a lift back.'

'Not convincing.'

Fergal chuckled. 'Maybe not. But what is up? You look like a dreich Sabbath, as Aunt Morag would say.'

'Row with Sam,' Ceri said.

'Well – what about?'

'Business of yours?' Ceri asked.

'No,' Fergal admitted, 'but he might listen to me when he wouldn't to you.'

'My father already offered.'

'Oh, come *on*!' Fergal said. 'Sam's not likely to heed him, What's the problem?'

'He took something from my room, that I was looking after for Ruth.' Ceri picked up a pebble and threw it towards the sea.

'Ruth?' Fergal said. He seemed to wait for her to say yes; but Ceri didn't see why she should. 'So what was it?' he asked.

Ceri looked at him sideways. 'What does it matter to you?'

'Leaving that aside for the moment,' Fergal said, 'if it was a seal skin, then I took it myself.'

Hard, cold rage swept through Ceri like a white flame; its strength surprised her. 'You *thief*!'

Fergal seemed undisturbed. 'If you call it stealing to take something back that was stolen in the first place, then yes.' He looked at her. 'I did tell you about having a family feeling with Euan.'

'I might have believed you if I'd known you meant it!'

'Oh, I meant it,' Fergal said. 'And I mean it now. I think.'

Ceri sighed. 'How did you find out I had the – skin?'

'Remember I came in for those French books? One fell down behind the bed,' Fergal said. 'And even then – I didn't believe it at first. What I was touching.'

'Would have thought you would be first to believe it,' Ceri said. 'Scottish and all that.'

'Well, yes,' Fergal said, with an edge of what was almost

desperation in his voice, 'but I've known Euan for years, and never had the least idea. And this is *here*. And *now*. Myths don't happen any more.'

'This one's only happening because we've seen it,' Ceri said.

'That doesn't make sense.'

'Does to me.' Ceri looked at him. 'It might have been any old seal skin – so what made you know it was Euan's?'

Fergal shook his head. 'I just knew. You understand? Oh yes, all right, never mind whatever I said about myths. It was like a ready-made answer. And besides – ' He shifted awkwardly in his place.

'What?'

'Euan was looking. Frantically, as if he needed . . .'

Fergal's voice died away for a moment. He cleared his throat. 'I met him on the beach. He said he'd lost something, wouldn't say what. Prowling up and down like – like a wild animal.'

'Yes.' Ceri said. 'I've seen him—'

'And then at Ruth's,' Fergal went on, 'I saw that cupboard, the way you looked at it. And she was looking at the keys.'

'So it was you took the key!' Ceri said.

Fergal nodded. 'She leaves the cottage door unlocked now and then. I looked in the cupboard when I had the chance, but it was empty, of course. So I left the key on the mat and went away.'

'Ruth gave – it – to me to look after,' Ceri said. She looked at Fergal. He had the seal skin. She'd have to apologise to Sam, for one thing. And for another . . . what should she tell Ruth? Whose side was Fergal on?

'What are we going to do?' she asked.

'We?' Fergal said. 'You don't come into it except by accident.'

'What do you mean?'

Fergal looked at her and said, 'You don't belong here. Nor does Ruth. I'm not having a couple of incomers taking over.'

Ceri swallowed. If he wanted it that way . . . 'What are you going to do with it, then?'

'Give it back to Euan, of course.'

'But –'

'But what?' Fergal asked irritably.

'He'll go away.' Ceri shut her eyes briefly. Imagine the sea shore without Euan.

'Maybe he will.' Fergal sighed, and said, 'It'll not be forever. Like I said, he was in these parts before ever your sister came here, let alone you. I mind him well enough.' Fergal chuckled suddenly. 'I mitched from school one time when I was small, and went out fishing with Euan. Had the best time ever – worth the shouting when I got home.'

'Was he younger then?' Ceri could not imagine Euan being any different from the way she knew him.

'And why for should he not be? He was about the age you are now when I was first acquent with him.'

'When you were first what?'

Fergal's eyebrows twitched upwards, but all he said was, 'When I first knew him.' He looked at her sideways. 'Will you see him before I do?'

'How should I know?' Ceri felt an indefinable, before-the-party twitch of excitement in her stomach, at the thought of seeing Euan. Why do the magazines always talk about hearts fluttering? All my heart does is pound along as usual. And my fingertips tingle – but they do that when someone squawks the chalk on the blackboard. 'I suppose I might,' she said.

'Aunt Morag says he's taking *Saltair* out again tomorrow. I thought I'd have a cook-up on the beach again. Same place as before. Tell Euan I'll be there if he wants to come by.'

'Won't he be wanting it sooner? Can't you take it to him now?'

'I'm due at the hotel.' Fergal stood up, and Ceri tipped her head back to look at him. He seemed very tall against the blue sky. 'If you see Euan,' he said, 'tell him I'll give it back to him tomorrow.'

She had forgotten he worked at the hotel. Ceri swallowed briefly, remembering the awful falling-off-a-cliff sensation of seeing two parts of her life collide; Mum and Dad, face to face.

'Do you see much of my father?' she asked. 'At The Shieling?'

'He's very popular,' Fergal said, as if that was an answer. 'Especially in the bar.'

'I might go back to America with him. He invited me.' Ceri's neck was beginning to ache. She looked straight ahead. Fergal's jeans had holes in them. 'What did you say?'

'You heard me,' Fergal said. 'Didn't you?'

'Maybe.' But Ceri did not want to admit that what she had heard him say was, 'Don't.'

'Are you coming?' Fergal asked.

'Where to?'

'Oh – back. Back to the house.'

'No. I'll stay here.' Ceri turned to face out to sea, and felt the noise of Fergal's car as he drove away: through the air or through the ground, she could not tell. The wind thrummed through the air until it felt like the inside of an organ pipe, with some vast music playing that Ceri was too small to hear. The pulse of the waves on the beach might have been the beat of blood inside her ears. Ceri stared as if her sight would stretch beyond the horizon. If this is the Atlantic, then America is over there. An imaginary land of skyscrapers, glossy and sleek with wealth. Could I make that real for me? Ceri stared at her own hands, her thumbs lined up against each other like mirror images. Real, unreal. Which is which?

Sixteen

A shadow fell across her hands, and she looked up to see Euan: as she had first seen him on the beach below the house, with the sun behind him. 'Euan,' she said.

'Ceri,' Euan replied, sounding oddly uncertain. He sat down beside her. 'How's Fergal?'

'All right . . . shouldn't he be?'

Euan chuckled. 'Not that I really need to know,' he said. 'But it starts a conversation. We parted on strange terms . . . Last time.'

Ceri couldn't look at his face. She found herself looking at his neck instead, the dip and angle of the skin where the collar-bone curved like a bird's wing into his breast bone. She wanted to reach out and touch him. 'You're a silkie,' she said.

Euan opened his mouth, hesitated, and said, 'Yes.'

'What – what does it feel like?'

'Nothing else on earth.' Euan sat very still.

Ceri lifted her hand. Lightly she touched the hollow between his two collar bones, and felt the pulse beating there like a wave under the skin.

'At the moment,' Euan said, 'it feels like being only half alive. Marooned between the tides.' It was warm in that sheltered place, in the sun: but he shivered.

'Fergal said—' Ceri began, and realised she was still touching Euan. She took her hand away. 'Fergal said, if you come to the hollow – you know the place – after taking *Saltair* out tomorrow, he'll be there with – it.'

Euan was so quiet she thought maybe he hadn't heard her. 'He took it from my room,' she said, a little louder. 'So as to give it back to you.'

At that Euan turned his head. 'And did you not ask for it back yourself?'

'He said I didn't belong. He didn't seem to think it was any of my business.' Ceri could hear the resentment seeping round the edges of her voice.

'He's not always right,' Euan said, and turned his face away again so that he was looking out to sea. Abruptly he said, 'Your father will be aboard *Saltair* tomorrow.'

'Oh.' Taken aback, Ceri thought frantically, should I tell him Dad knows? surely there won't be any – she stopped herself. Of course there won't be.

'Ruth's coming too,' Euan said, and before Ceri could think about that he went on, 'Fergal, you say Fergal's got it, and I'll have it tomorrow?'

'Yes.'

'*Glory*.' Euan took a deep breath, and tipped his head back. Ceri wanted to reach out and touch him again. I love you, she thought. But she said nothing.

Euan said, very quietly, 'I know.' And looked at her. For the first time since she had known him, he was fumbling for words.

'I can't, Ceri,' he said. 'Not you.'

She blurted out, 'Couldn't you even try?' and heard how foolish the question sounded even as it escaped her lips. Euan didn't laugh. He did smile, very briefly. 'It doesn't work like that,' he said.

'So why does it work for Ruth?' Ceri asked bitterly, shaken by the wave of feeling that crashed down on her.

'Don't hate her,' was all he said.

'Why should I?' Ceri answered, flattening her voice to push it past the tears that were all she really wanted to let loose. 'It's just – I never had a chance – all people see is—' She put her hands to her ears, as if that would stop her saying it.

Euan turned, and put his hands on her shoulders so hard that it hurt. 'Don't ever say that again. Seeing is nothing to do with it.' He stopped short, as if English had suddenly become a foreign language and he had forgotten how to speak it. He looked at his hands, and lifted them from her shoulders. Then he stood up. 'Ruth is where I belong.'

'Then why.' Ceri's voice wouldn't do what she said. 'Then. Why did you kiss *me*?'

'I don't know – no!' Euan said. 'Not true.' He looked at her. 'We understand each other, don't we? In your underwater land.'

Ceri nodded silently. Euan said, 'We're too alike not to feel – something. But . . .' His eyes were like windows on to a wide sky where the north wind blew. 'I'm sorry. Do you believe me?'

'Have to,' Ceri said, and watched Euan smile again.

He walked away before she could collect her wits to say anything else.

The sun went in. Ceri watched the cloud shadows drive the

myriad glitter of light from the waves, as if they tried to silence – what had Fergal called it? – *ceol na mara*. The music of the sea. I should have said more to Euan. He doesn't understand, he doesn't realise. She crushed her face down on her knees, until the pressure on her eyelids made purple and green clouds swell and dance against the darkness. Euan Euan Euan . . . She said the words aloud. Nobody answered.

When she walked into the lounge Sam went upstairs and into his own room. Her mother, sitting at the kitchen table with her head propped on her hands over a cup of coffee, looked up. 'Have you and Sam been fighting again?'

'Arguing,' Ceri said.

'What about? Not whatever it was you lost?'

Ceri sighed. She was so *tired* of all this continually having to talk about things. 'No, not this time. Didn't he tell you?'

'He wouldn't,' her mother said. 'He said it was between you and him.'

'But he used to tell you everything,' Ceri said. 'Even when it wasn't his business.'

'Yes,' her mother said. 'He's growing up, perhaps.'

Ceri pulled out a chair and sat down. 'What's that got to do with it?'

'Fighting his own battles, perhaps . . . I don't know.'

Ceri leaned forward and rested her head on her clenched fists. 'If that means growing up I must be about ninety.' She closed her eyes. 'Mum, what am I going to *do*?'

Of course she wasn't going to hear what Mum said with her eyes shut. She looked up again.

'Is there anything – particular – you want my advice about?'

her mother asked. 'Because you know I'm, um, biased. In some areas.'

In other words, keep off the Paul subject. Ceri said untruthfully, 'No, nothing in particular. Just in general.'

'You could try,' her mother said, 'stopping fighting? Growing up is one thing. Maturity's another . . . I still get the urge to fight. Too often.' She got up from the table and put her empty cup in the sink. 'How about a trip to Ardnamurchan?'

Crunch, Ceri thought. Hear the subject changing. 'What's there?' she asked. Let's go along with it.

'A lighthouse, some good views, and the westernmost point of the British mainland. It's a nature reserve, I think.'

'OK. I'll come.'

The afternoon and evening passed in a strangely peaceful way. Peaceful but uneasy, as if the cease-fire were only temporary, and more fragile than they thought. Ceri tried to find a moment to apologise to Sam. He came out to Ardnamurchan, but only talked to Mum; and Ceri, getting no reply from him, began to do the same. As for Mum, she seemed to have neither the energy nor the inclination to tell them to snap out of it and behave like normal human beings.

When they got back to the house, there was the usual moment of small chaos in the hall as everyone kicked off shoes, or dropped bags. Then Sam went into his room, and Ceri, on the way to her own, looked back briefly to see her mother stopped between the two, with her eyes closed and her arms straight down by her side. She looks so tired. Between the two of us, me and Sam, me and Dad. Hastily Ceri turned away and shut the door.

Ceri's watch stopped some time after lunch the next day, and she didn't realise until she noticed the panel of sunlight angling from the lounge wall to the glass table. Her little wooden seal gleamed in it as if lit from within.

'What's the time?' she asked.

Only Sam was in the room, and he didn't answer. With a sigh as audible as she could make it, Ceri went into the kitchen to look at the clock on the microwave.

'Half past three!' She snatched the seaward door open and hurled herself down the path. On the ridge above the sea her mother was standing, turning something over and over in her hands. Ceri glanced at it. A packet of cigarettes. Unopened. Her mother looked up guiltily, and put it into her pocket.

'Where are you going?'

'Along the beach to meet Fergal.' Ceri lifted herself up and down on her toes, itching to be off.

Mum nodded. 'Not with – Paul?'

'Would I tell you if I was?'

'Probably not.' Her mother looked at her. 'Are you going to – ?'

'Don't,' Ceri said. 'Don't ask me. Whatever it is. I don't know.'

There was a long silence. Then her mother crushed her hands together as if to squelch – anger? frustration? and said, 'Have a good time, then.'

Ceri scrunched across the shingle wondering whether her mother meant it. You can open your mouth and out the polite words come, because they always do, even if you would rather be half a continent away and doing something else. She scrambled over the rocks at the foot of the headland, where once Euan had sat singing to the seals. The tide was on the way in, hiding the long stony tongue of land that stretched out into the water. Above her head the clouds streamed in the wind, shadows flickering over sea and land. It was almost like a time-lapse film: would she get to the end of her journey and find that years had passed?

Something flashed like a gull's wing on the water. Ceri strained her eyes: would that be *Saltair*? If it was, then Euan wasn't running the engine; never mind anyone's stomach. The yacht was coming towards her, heeling over, scudding across the water with the water creaming under the bows, the sails curved white and brilliant in the sunshine. It was *Saltair*. Heading back towards Kinloch and the end of the trip.

Ceri felt as if she was watching a film. Without sound, of course; just the noise of the wind in her hearing aids. She sat on her heels to wait; but what she was waiting for she couldn't have said. Now there were three parts of her life close enough to collide; Euan, Ruth, her father. And she couldn't do a thing.

Soon Ceri could see Euan standing on the counter at the stern, one hand twisted round the line that secured the life-raft. He was steering with one foot on the tiller, and Ruth was standing in the steering-well; Ceri could see her hair bright against the blue sea. The passengers were sitting casually in the space in front of the mast. All of them were men, all in the green and brown clothes she associated with glossy magazines in the waiting-rooms of countless audiology units. Nobody seemed to have bothered with buoyancy aids, but perhaps that was their own affair. Someone was holding a bottle.

There was her father. She couldn't mistake his height, that way he had of holding his head up. Even at a distance he looked as if he were in charge, his hands moving to mark the emphasis of his words, and now the yacht was close enough for Ceri to see a ripple of movement through the group; he must have made them laugh or something. Her father was getting to his feet, going astern – heading for the cabin.

Ceri's gaze shifted to the stern. Ruth was standing beside Euan now, and his arm was round her shoulders. Paul negotiated the steps down to the cabin without a pause, and reappeared with another bottle in his hands. On the steps up from the steering well he stopped.

There was absolutely no way Ceri could see whether anyone was speaking. But her father was so still. Maybe he was using the silent angry glare that he had turned on Fergal that night at The Shieling. He didn't like Euan . . . and Euan – what had Euan said about her father? *I hated his guts.* Or something like that.

Her father went forward again, and was still moving when Euan put the tiller hard over. Her father swayed alarmingly on the tilting deck, caught hold of the rail on the cabin roof, and turned in one abrupt movement to face astern. Euan was kissing Ruth. Paul stood there, quite still, watching; and then returned to his colleagues and sat down. A second later the yacht swung round again, out into the middle of the loch. Ceri could see Euan's back and Ruth's, close together.

It won't be long before they come ashore. If Ruth is with Euan now then she'll be with him when he meets Fergal. When Fergal gives the seal skin back. Ceri found herself biting her knuckles. Explanations, recriminations, arguments. Could she bear any more of them? *Do I want to see Euan if – if he goes back to the sea? If he stays with Ruth? Whatever happens?*

Hours must have passed. Ceri thought, I wish I could see into the future. Just for once. One tiny glimpse. With a sigh she stood up. The future. It'll arrive sooner or later, and then I'll know.

As soon as she had a long view of the land, she saw someone running towards her. Sam. Well, he won't want to speak to me. But he came straight to her, stopped, and stood there gulping his breath back.

'Ceri,' he said, 'Ceri, have you seen your father? Where is he?'

'I don't know.' Ceri looked deliberately away from him, but Sam moved round her and said, 'Look, so maybe we aren't on speaking terms and I'm sorry, but whatever you think this is important.' He had articulated every word so that she heard it first time.

'OK, it's important.'

Still Sam hesitated. 'Friends? Or at least – not at war?'

Ceri grinned. 'Truce. Anyway I should apologise to you, I'll tell you later . . . but I still don't know where Dad is. Ashore somewhere and gone back to his hotel, I expect . . . why, what's up?'

Normally at a question like this Sam would scuff his feet and talk to his trainers. This time, looking into Ceri's face, he said, 'He's ashore all right. He turned up at the house. I mean, not to talk. First I knew was his car, came down that track like he was driving Formula 1, straight through the gate. Lucky Mum left it open when she went out for the shopping.'

'Where were you?'

'Watching a video, but that doesn't matter. I got up when I heard the car. Anyway – he came running in through the upstairs door, and straight down the stairs and asked for you, "Where's Ceri?" just like that.' Sam paused. 'He was in a real rage. I mean – nothing he said, but I could tell, just the way he was moving. I said I thought you might have gone to meet Ruth or Euan and he sort of hissed, and this is the thing, he was in the kitchen by then and he just closed his hand round John's air-gun and took it with him, I'm not even sure he knew he had it.'

'Didn't you stop him?' Ceri asked.

'I never got a chance, it happened faster than telling it,' Sam said. 'He went out by the other door and running round the house – he can't half move, for someone wearing all that posh gear and then I heard the car go off. And I was supposed to be looking after that gun, there'll be trouble . . .'

The gun. He knows about guns. The gunner. He can use them. Ceri blinked and shook her head, as if something had hit her. I ought to remember something, try to remember . . . she stood there looking blankly at Sam's anxious face. Something else. He's taken the car. Well you can't hide a car like that round here. 'Which way did he go?' she asked.

'I don't know,' Sam said. 'Somewhere towards that place with the long line of rocks, I think, he must have taken the car off the road. He'll ruin the suspension, and Ceri –' He stopped. 'I don't know what to do.'

Ceri all but choked as the words finally put themselves together inside her head.

> The very first shot that ever he shoots
> Will kill . . .

I mustn't tell Sam *that*. She smiled, trying to reassure him. 'I'll go and look for him, the car'll be easy to find,' she said. 'Don't worry. I'll get it back.' She wondered if she sounded convincing.

'Be careful,' Sam said dubiously.

'Oh Sam, I don't need to be careful. Go and watch your video.' Ceri waited to see Sam start on his way back to the house. Then she began to run. Perspiration prickled between her shoulder blades. Quick, quick – but surely I don't really need to hurry? This is here, and now, after all. Surely my father – my father! – can't really . . . surely?

There was a fresh tyre-mark in a bare patch of sandy earth. He'd come this way. She careered down a long shallow slope and past the ruined wall of a sheep-fold; in its shelter was the car, the driver's door open and the keys still swinging in the ignition. Another slope. Ceri tripped on a tussock of grass, almost fell, and recovered herself. Come on. Keep going. She reached the top and looked towards the headland.

There was her father, running. Breathlessly Ceri followed him. At last she was in sight of the beach. A smell of fish frying came to her nose, and her mouth watered. So Fergal must be down there somewhere. She stopped to get her breath back, and saw Euan and Ruth come walking across the shingle. Fergal went forward to meet them. He had a carrier bag in one hand, and swung it as casually as if it were the day's shopping; but Ceri knew it held the seal skin.

Euan's arm was across Ruth's shoulders. Ceri's mind flicked into flashback: the memory of the feel of Euan's arms round her own body. Her father's arm across her shoulders. She swallowed, and looked again. Ruth leaned over and kissed Euan.

Her father stopped still for one split second, and ran on towards the cliff edge with long stiff angry strides. She saw he had the gun.

The wind filled Ceri's ears, its roar muffled, but still loud enough to drown out other sounds. Her cry was blown back in her throat. She dragged more air into her lungs, and dived towards her father. She was never quite sure if she heard the shot, or only felt the recoil in his arm: then she skidded sickeningly on the dry grass, held for one desperate moment, and went over the edge, taking the gun with her, dropping like a stone into deep water.

Seventeen

The cold shock of it drove all the breath from Ceri's lungs. Her feet touched the bottom, and she kicked up frantically. This was no underwater music in her ears, but an unfamiliar, threatening roar. She could see nothing but a whirl of bubbles, didn't even know whether she was looking up to the surface.

Something warm nudged against her. She grabbed at it, then pushed it away in a panic. Suppose it was her father, fallen in as well, dead and drowned and coming past her? But it came back towards her: her fingers slipped on something soft, and suddenly, unbelievably, Euan's voice rang like a bell through the roaring waters. 'Ceri. You're safe. I've got you.' With an explosion of light they came up into the air. Ceri, the breath whooping down her throat, reached round and clung on. She blinked the salt out of her eyes, and lifted her head. Her hands were touching – no, they couldn't be; what she saw was Euan, treading water beside her. His hair was slicked back from his face, and the scar on his forehead showed clearly. She put her hand on it, and buried her face in his shoulder. 'Oh, Euan.'

'I'm all right,' Euan said in her ear.

'The gunner,' she said.

Euan said nothing. They hung between waves, the water swaying round them. Time stretched, or shrunk, she wasn't sure which.

At last, or was it only a moment later, Euan said, 'Ceri. Come on.'

Ceri took a deep breath. 'Let's go away,' she said. One last try. 'Take me with you.'

He shook his head. 'Can't be done.'

No good. And the others were still there, ashore. Ceri turned wearily, letting the waves slap her sideways. 'I'm too tired to swim.'

'Take my arm, then. And hold your breath.' Euan turned his back, and slipped under the water with a movement like someone pulling up the hood of a coat. Blindly Ceri held on, feeling the undersea currents tugging at her, and Euan's arm – or was it an arm? – warm under her hand, as if there was a fire beneath his skin. I've felt this before, she thought. Touching the seal. I remember it now. I suppose I'll forget, some day.

They surfaced again in the tumble of the breaking waves. Ceri staggered to her feet, and looked round in time to see Euan shaking himself free of something. He walked ashore with it trailing from his hand, but let it fall on the shingle, and crouched against the slope of the hollow, dripping wet, with his hair plastered so flat down that Ceri could see the shape of his skull.

She was still ankle-deep in water when there was a spatter of stones, and Paul Schaefer, half-running and half-slithering down the slope of the headland, came to a halt beside Fergal. She stepped on to the beach, stumbled, and recovered her balance. At the same moment her father got his breath back, shouted 'What did you go do a dam-fool thing like that for?' and hit out. Ceri felt his hand smack across the side of her face, and then someone dragged her out of his reach. 'Let *go*!' she said, and turned to face her father. 'You were going to kill him. Was I supposed to let you?' The sound of her words came cracked and broken to her ears; the water must have got into her hearing aids.

Her father snapped, 'Don't talk crap. The bloody thing wasn't loaded. Anyway – since when was anyone killed with an air-gun at that range?' He stopped, breathing hard, and stared at Euan. 'You,' he said. 'You want both of them, don't you? Just leave them alone. You hear?'

Ruth stepped forward from behind Ceri. 'Just one thing. These are our lives. You. Leave us alone.'

He stared at her, the cold anger waiting to be unleashed. 'You're *my* daughters.'

Ceri backed away and sat down. Her face was stinging. He hit me. And he said he never would. She curled up with her arms round her knees.

Ruth said coolly, 'If I'm your daughter, then give me what I want.'

'You can have it,' he said. 'I always told you, you can have anything.'

'Freedom,' Ruth said.

There was a long silence. Then her father said, 'You I do not understand. You could have anything. *Anything*. Isn't that freedom?'

What was it Ruth had said? Being his daughter left no room for anything else. Ceri shivered. The other conversation seemed to be taking place at an immense distance. I thought he liked me. Enough to want to be my father. Or did he only want –

'If you won't understand I can't tell you,' Ruth said.

Or did he only want me to be his daughter? Like his suit, and his car. His, and nothing else . . . she looked up.

Paul was standing by Euan, looking down at him. He said, 'What'll you take to leave her alone?'

Euan looked up, and bared his teeth. 'Don't tempt me.' The two men looked at each other, silently hostile. Euan said again, cold and dangerous, 'Don't.'

Paul looked at him. 'I guess I owe you something for pulling Ceri out. Fine. You can have Ruth. If that's the way she wants it.' He turned away, and Ceri, reading the face and lips as well as hearing the words, saw a glint of vicious fury that her father probably never knew he showed.

Will it always be like that? Hearing him say one thing, seeing him mean another? She closed her eyes and rested her head on her knees.

Was that the scrunch of feet on pebbles she heard, or the water in her ears? Faintly she heard her father say, 'You come back with me, kid. Okay? November.'

How would you keep him from losing his temper? Would you lead your life the way he wants you to? Would it *be* your life?

'Ceri?' she heard her father say.

Speak now. Speak now. What's the phrase? Or forever hold your peace. Ceri screwed her eyes tighter closed, pushed her face a little harder against her knees. I could have anything. Ceri felt her heart pounding, pounding.

'*Ceri*.'

The darkness behind her eyes flickered. Ceri gritted her

teeth. If he wants me enough he'll wait.

When at last she opened her eyes he was gone.

There was a smell of burning. Fergal stepped forward and moved the pan, with its black and curling cargo, away from the fire.

'You all right?' he asked. Not much to ask, but what else was there to say?

Ceri nodded. 'The gun's at the bottom of the sea. Sorry.'

'Uncle John won't mind,' Fergal said. 'Not about the gun. Anyway, it won't go far, I know this stretch of shore. I'll come back and get it tomorrow morning when the tide's out.' He sluiced the frying-pan out with sea-water. 'He might want to press charges about your father's taking it.'

'Never mind that,' Ruth said. 'Euan could press charges. It was him was shot at.'

'I should have remembered,' Ceri said, shivering. 'I saw John MacInnes take the pellets away. I might have saved all the fuss. I might as well not have bothered.'

'The rage he was in . . .' Ruth began.

'Leave it,' Euan said, leaning back wearily against the side of the hollow. 'I'm not going into any court. Let him go. Not as if he'll be this side of the ocean for long.'

There was silence. Ceri got up, and moved forward slowly until the seal skin was at her feet. 'Didn't he see?' she said, wonderingly. 'Didn't he notice?'

'Most likely not,' Fergal said, walking up beside her. 'He isn't the sort to notice things. In any case he didn't stop to look. He came pelting down here at once.' He looked at Ceri. 'He must care something for you.'

'Not enough,' Ceri said, hearing her own voice as she had

done all the others, hollow and distant. Inside the electronic intricacies of her hearing aids the sea-water must be slowly drying, crystallising into salt and jamming up the works, as once long ago a virus had etched itself into the coiled chambers of her inner ear, picking off certain frequencies with the random destructiveness of a meteor-shower in space. Ceri put her hands to her ears as if she had to hold her head together.

Fergal stooped and picked up the seal skin. He shook it and held it, still shiny wet, towards Euan. 'Here you are, *caraid*.'

Euan reached out, but it was Ruth who stepped forward and took the skin from Fergal's hands. She glanced at Euan, and with a sudden stiff movement flung the skin at the fire.

'*No!*' Euan shouted: but before Ruth could even turn towards him, he screamed.

It was the most dreadful sound Ceri had ever heard. Without stopping to think she walked to the fire and picked the skin out, and the flames wrapped round her hands like burning gloves. She plunged forward; Fergal caught her, and wrapped the wet seal skin round her fingers. She stumbled away from the fire and leaned against him for a moment.

'All right!' she said breathlessly. 'I'm not burnt.'

He looked down at her. 'Good.'

Suddenly everything seemed very quiet. Ceri said, 'What did you call Euan, just now?'

'*Caraid*? It means, kinsman. He is, you know.'

'I know. Ceri looked at him. 'Go away, Fergal,' she said. 'Just till – oh, I don't know. Please. We'll be all right.'

'Okay, I'll go,' he said. 'But I'll see you later.'

'All right,' she said again.

Fergal went away; slowly, glancing back over his shoulder.

Ceri watched him as long as she could, so as to avoid looking at the other two.

Ruth was beside Euan, her arms round his shoulders. His face was buried in the hollow of her neck. Slowly Ceri crossed the shingle towards them, dropped the seal skin, and knelt down at their side. After a moment Ruth and Euan each put an arm round her. For a little while it was just the three of them huddled together at the water's edge. Ceri looked up at last, in time to see Ruth say, 'What are you going to do? Where will you go?'

Euan said again, 'Leave it.'

Slowly Ruth stood up. Ceri could barely read the words on her lips.

'You've got it back now,' Ruth said. 'You can go where you like now. But I don't want to lose you.' And she walked away. Euan shuddered, as if someone had walked over his grave, and his arm moved across Ceri's shoulders. Ceri rubbed her eyes, and Euan shifted his footing and stood up. He picked up the seal skin where it lay crumpled on the pebbles at his feet, and the shudder went through him again.

'Euan?' Ceri said, but he didn't seem to hear her. He stood twisting the skin between his hands and staring out across the loch where the sunlight leapt and sparkled on the waves: *gait na mara*, the laughter of the sea. Then suddenly he hugged the seal skin to himself as fiercely as Ceri had held on to him in the water, burying his face in its folds. Ceri looked away, feeling as if she shouldn't be there.

When she looked again Euan was folding the skin carefully into a small neat bundle. He knelt down by Ceri again and said, 'Here.'

'What?'

'Take it,' he said. 'Take it away. Look after it. Sleep under it, walk on it, hang it on the wall, anything you like.'

'Anything?'

He grinned uncertainly. 'Perhaps not swimming.'

'Where could I? The Serpentine? I'd end up in the zoo.'

Something like a laugh came from between Euan's lips. 'Look after it,' he said again.

'Until you want it back?' Her mouth was dry. Fear? Hope?

Euan stood up. 'I don't want to lose Ruth any more than she wants to lose me,' he said. 'Take it away, Ceri. So I won't have to decide.'

'Will you want it back?' she asked again. 'Ever?'

After a long pause Euan said, 'Maybe. One day.' He turned to follow the way Ruth had taken.

'Euan! Euan – don't go.' Ceri felt as if she must be screaming; but the voice she heard was what you would expect when your mouth was so dry you could hardly speak.

Euan may have heard her; at any rate he paused. But he did not look back. He went on, his feet dragging and slipping on the loose shingle as if he was very tired.

Ceri sat there, hugging the skin to herself. The world was miles away, and she was on her own. There didn't seem to be anything she could do, not even cry. What good would it do? The waves were empty, but as the wind blew past her ears she imagined she heard a faint low singing. Her wet clothes were cooling on her, clammy even in the sunshine. At last she got up, took a few uncertain steps, and stumbled inland towards the house.

Mum was standing by the gate. 'Ceri, love,' she said. 'Come in and get dry.'

Ceri looked up. 'How did you know?'

'Fergal came by and told us.' She hesitated. 'Michael's here – back from Eindhoven. He hired a car – we'll go home the day after tomorrow, the way we planned, but in two cars as far as Glasgow.'

'Oh,' Ceri said. What else could she say? Somewhere out there the world crept a little closer again. Michael. Sam. Cars and motorways. Home. 'Sam must be pleased,' she said vaguely.

'He is.'

Ceri leaned against the doorpost and closed her eyes. Had she ever been this tired? 'Actually,' she said, 'so am I.'

Mum said, nervously, as if she was dreading the reply, 'Fergal told me Paul was there.'

'He was.' Ceri went indoors and began climbing the stairs. 'I'm staying here,' she said, and didn't look back to see how Mum took it: but then Mum ran upstairs, hugged her, and went away again before Ceri could get her breath back.

Next day. Ceri was leaning on the fence and watching John MacInnes's collies, when Fergal came to stand beside her. 'Hi.'

'Hallo.' She looked round. 'No car?'

'Silencer's bust.'

'You mean it had one?' Ceri looked at herself laughing, and thought, this time yesterday – how can I laugh? 'When I'm in London,' she said, 'I shan't see a blancmange without thinking of the pink peril.'

'Hey,' Fergal said, 'alliteration's my line.'

Ceri glanced at him, and caught him grinning at her. 'Superior Scot,' she said.

He wrinkled his nose. 'So, you asked for it. Arrogant American.'

'You shut up. I'm English. So go and alliterate that, Fergal MacInnes.'

She had thought he would laugh, but instead he looked at her seriously. 'I start at Sussex in the autumn.'

'Good luck.'

'Thanks, but that's not just what I meant. It's not so far from London, is it?'

'Not very,' she said.

'Well then.'

They looked at each other. Ceri said, 'You do know what's been going on . . .'

Fergal said, 'I know well enough. But we can have each other's addresses without the world ending – can't we?'

It was the very minute before they left. The phone rang. Mum answered it, wrote something down, and came towards Ceri. 'That was Fergal MacInnes,' she said. 'He gave me his address; but there wasn't any message. Well, not really.'

'What do you mean, not really?' Ceri asked.

'It was just a word.'

'But which *one*?'

'Enigmatic,' Mum replied, and when Ceri laughed she said, 'I suppose you must know what he's talking about.'

'Alliteration,' Ceri said. She picked up her suitcase and took it outside. 'Okay if I sit in the back?'

'All yours till Glasgow,' Mum said, so Ceri climbed in and made herself comfortable. They bounced out along the farm track and waited. Sam was taking the key back to John

MacInnes – a brief dazzle of fluorescence as he dashed past to join Michael in the other car. Up the slope; at the top, a glimpse of Ruth's cottage. The sea was behind them now. Ceri fixed her gaze on the grey rock and heather, and willed herself not to look round.

Euan chose. Unless he left his options open when he said, maybe one day. He chose Ruth. And I chose Mum after all. So here I am. Neither deaf nor hearing; just myself . . . going home. Keep going, Ceri.

After a while she found a clean sheet in her sketch-pad and began to write.

> *Dear Sir,*
> *I would like to learn sign language. Is it too late? . . .*

The two cars swung down the road, east and southward. Framed by the windows, the slopes of the mountains swooped and fell, making their silent gestures of beauty against the sky.

WATERBOUND

Jane Stemp

The City is a place of rules, a place where Admin is always watching ... a place where there is no room to be different.

Under the City, the river flows from light into dark, into an unknown place. A place which hides a secret. Something forbidden – out of sight and out of mind.

There Gem finds the Waterbound, the children the City forgot. She joins in their fight to be part of the world she knows.

Why are they underground? Is there a way out?

ESCAPE

June Oldham

Are there some secrets that can't be told?

Magdalen has finished school and is about to leave home. Freedom at last, final and total escape.

But her father has other plans.

So she runs away, away from him and their terrible secret. With her goes Greg, a stranger, and gradually through him the power of the secret is broken.

Together they conquer Magdalen's past and she faces the future with hope.

A deeply moving story about a girl escaping from incest.

Another Hodder Children's book

THE FATED SKY

Henrietta Branford

There was a dragon in the sky the night before the stranger came. It flamed across the red west from the cliffs to the black road of the sea. It did not speak to me. But I feared it.

After the death of her father and brothers in a viking raid, Ran is alone. Alone and afraid. Travelling by sledge across a snowy headland to take part in the winter sacrifice, her future is uncertain.

Her fate lies in the hands of Vigut, a cruel stranger who brings nothing but fear and death. Her life at the mercy of an evil magician. Her destiny in the love of a travelling musician. But where the journey ends is up to her . . .